Praise for the novels of Bella Andre

"Sensual, empowered stories enveloped in heady romance."
—*Publishers Weekly*

"This is such a great story about loss, the rebuilding of lives
and the emotions that can rip it all apart. Readers will look
forward to more from this talented author."
—*RT Book Reviews* on *Can't Help Falling in Love*

"Bella Andre writes warm, sexy contemporary romance
that always gives me a much needed pick-me-up.
Reading one of her books is truly a pleasure."
—Maya Banks, *New York Times* bestselling author

"Andre is simply a wonder. With each entry in the fantastic
Sullivans series, her writing is kicked up a notch…. Andre is
at the top of her game!"
—*RT Book Reviews* on *Come a Little Bit Closer*, Top Pick

"Lovable characters, sizzling chemistry
and poignant emotion."
—Christie Ridgway, *USA TODAY* bestselling author

"I'm hooked on the Sullivans!"
—Marie Force, bestselling author of *Falling for Love*

BELLA ANDRE

The Way You Look Tonight

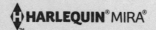

Recycling programs
for this product may
not exist in your area.

ISBN-13: 978-0-7783-1730-2

The Way You Look Tonight

Harlequin MIRA/September 2014
First published by Bella Andre

Copyright © 2013 by Oak Press, LLC.

Printed in U.S.A.

Dear Reader,

I have been writing about the Sullivan family for two years and loving every single second of creating emotional love stories about these sexy heroes and strong heroines! Thank you for being the most amazing readers in the world! Your emails, tweets, Facebook and Goodreads messages have made me laugh, tear up and appreciate writing romance more than ever.

In fact, *you* are the reason I'm writing more stories about the Sullivans! After the first eight San Francisco Sullivans found their happily-ever-afters, so many readers requested more Sullivans that I'm thrilled to present you with the Seattle branch of the family. Over the course of the next five books, I can't wait to introduce you to Rafe, Mia, Ian, Dylan and Adam, and their parents, Max and Claudia Sullivan. Of course, along the way we'll peek back in on the lives of the first eight Sullivans and their mother in San Francisco.

I should also note that if this is your first time reading about the Sullivans, you can easily read each book as a stand-alone—and there is a Sullivan family tree available on my website (www.bellaandre.com), so you can see how the books connect together.

I sincerely hope you love getting to know my supersexy P.I. Rafe Sullivan…and the woman he's about to realize he can't live without.

Happy reading,

Bella Andre

The Way You Look Tonight

One

Some days, Rafe Sullivan hated his job.

The elegantly dressed woman seated in front of him had tears streaming down her face, and her once-flawless makeup was ruined by the black streams of mascara tracking down her cheeks. Rafe slid the box of tissues closer to her, but she was too busy sobbing and clutching the photos he'd just given her to notice.

In each of the dozen pictures, his client's CEO husband was with a different woman. Brunettes, blondes and redheads were all represented. The only thing they shared in common was cup size, as each of the women was very well-endowed, including the young wife sitting in Rafe's office.

"That bastard!" she spat between sobs. "He swore he would never cheat. He said I was *everything* to him. During our wedding vows, he stood up in front of my family and told me I was the true love of his life." She lifted her gaze from the pictures, her eyes so full of pain. "Why couldn't he be faithful? Is it because I'm not as pretty as these women?"

Seven years ago, when Rafe had decided to leave the

police force and open up his own investigation firm, he'd been full of high ideals. Justice. Truth. That was what he'd been after. He now had half a dozen people working for him, and was widely considered to run the best P.I. firm in Washington State.

But how the hell had it come to this? He used to go into every case with an open mind. After all, how high could the statistics be in favor of infidelity? Fifty percent was high, he'd figured. Sixty percent would have been nuts.

He hadn't imagined a world in which 100 percent of the people he investigated were up to no good.

Somewhere along the way, Rafe's reputation for discovering whether or not high-profile men and women were cheating—and they always were—had eclipsed the number of his other investigative cases. He'd been unable to justify turning down these pricey jobs when he had a staff depending on him for salaries and benefits.

Though he'd been doing this for almost a decade, Rafe had never figured out how to numb himself to the moment when he handed his client the pictures he and his staff had taken of infidelity in action. He couldn't help but feel that he was at least partly responsible for their tears.

But, most of all, he hated the way the women moved all too quickly from anger to blaming themselves.

"This is not your fault," he said in a gentle voice.

He would like to have told his client that she was easily as beautiful as the women her husband had cheated with, and might even have reached out to touch her hand in comfort, but hard-won experience had taught him he couldn't even do that.

Comfort and much-needed compliments could be too easily mistaken for something more. He'd only been stupid enough to go down that road once, had known better than to start anything with one of his ex-clients, but she'd been persistent and pretty...and he'd been tired and just plain stupid. Boy, had *that* been a major screwup.

Now, though he wished he could do more to help his client, all he could do was hand her the tissues.

She finally plucked one from the box to wipe away her tears and running mascara. "I *trusted* him." Her voice was little more than a whisper now. "How will I ever be able to trust anyone again?"

Rafe knew she was waiting for him to assure her that not everyone was bad, that there were still some good guys out there. But after seven years of catching every cheater in the Pacific Northwest with their pants down, all he could do was remind her, "You have good instincts. That's why you came to me, isn't it?"

She nodded, her eyes finally drying. Thank God.

"Just keep trusting your instincts."

She seemed to think about his advice for a moment before taking a deep breath and wiping the rest of her tears away. "Yes, you're right, that's exactly what I need to do. Trust myself instead of anyone else. And right now my instincts are telling me to take my scumbag husband for absolutely *everything* he's worth." Renewed life glittered in her eyes as thoughts of revenge took hold.

His client had gone from anguish to self-blame to revenge all in the span of five minutes. It was only 10:00 a.m. He had seven more hours of this to look forward to.

She stood up and smoothed out her silk dress, stained with teardrops. "I can't thank you enough for your help, Mr. Sullivan."

He wished she hadn't had anything to thank him for as he shook her hand. "Good luck with everything."

"My soon-to-be ex-husband is the one who's going to be needing luck on his side," she assured him, before adding, "and I'll be sure to recommend you to my girlfriends." Cynicism now overshadowed her youthful beauty. "I'm sure most of them will be needing your services, too." She was halfway to his door when she turned back to him. "Do you know what hurts most of all? Even more than knowing that he was sleeping with other women? Even more than being lied to?"

Fortunately, Rafe knew it was a rhetorical question, so he simply waited for her to continue.

"He obviously didn't think I'd have the smarts or the nerve to find out what he was doing. If he wanted so badly to end our marriage, if he knew he didn't love me anymore, he should have been brave enough to just man up and tell me to my face." Her eyes narrowed. "But he didn't even have enough respect for me to do that."

As soon as she left his office, Rafe sank back on his leather couch and ran a hand over his face. And that was how his sister, Mia, found him a few minutes later when she burst into his office.

"I swear," she said, "the best-looking babes in the world come out of your office, and they're always wearing the most gorgeous and expensive shoes, too. Another rich guy screwing around on his trophy wife, huh?"

Rafe didn't bother to open his eyes. Or to acknowledge the question Mia already knew the answer to. Instead, he said, "If you're here to ask if you can take my Ducati for a ride, the answer is, and always will be, no." Lord only knew what his impulsive sister would do to his motorcycle if he let her have the keys, even for fifteen minutes. Besides, if she hurt herself by driving too fast or too wildly, his parents would kill him.

"Well, you certainly need some cheering up today, don't you?" He could hear her grinning even without looking at her. "Lucky for you, that's why I'm here."

Finally, he opened one eye. "Whatever you've got up your sleeve today, I'm not up for it. Try me again in six months."

"Trust me, this is going to make everything better. I promise."

Mia reached into her big red leather bag, something he guessed cost nearly as much as his motorcycle, and pulled out a piece of paper. Though he had never indicated he was in the market for a summer house, she'd been telling him about various lake properties for the past several months, emailing him pictures and handing him flyers when they were over at their parents' house for a meal. The constant barrage of lake house listings had got him thinking which, he knew, was entirely Mia's intent.

A couple of months away from crying, jilted trophy wives and cheating captains of industry?

Sounded like heaven.

His siblings all loved their work, especially Mia. She was so good at selling real estate that she'd opened her own brokerage well before she'd hit her thirties. His brother Adam had never seen a historic house he didn't want to rehab. Ian, the oldest Seattle Sullivan, made millions while he slept. And their brother Dylan had been sailing since before he could walk, so it made perfect sense that he was building some of the best boats out on the water.

Only Rafe was stuck with a successful business that was draining the life out of him, one day at a time.

"I don't need another house," Rafe muttered.

He closed his eyes again, settling deeper into his couch and kicking his feet up on the coffee table. Instead of making an irritated comment, or pushing his feet off the table, Mia let silence fall between them. Frankly, the silence worried him more than anything, given that his sister was not known for her deeply meditative states. Rather, she was the perfect combination of the Tasmanian devil and a whirling dervish. He was trying to muster up the energy to put a stop to whatever it was she was planning, when something sharp hit him between the eyes.

"Ow! What the hell, Mia?" There was a paper airplane on his lap, its nose bent from the impact with his forehead.

"Just look at it already. I know how busy you are consoling weeping women all day, and I wouldn't bother you unless it was really important." She pointed at the paper airplane. "Trust me, *this* is important."

Knowing it was best to humor her so that he could get on with his shitty day, Rafe unfolded the airplane. There wasn't much printed on the listing page apart from the fuzzy picture at the top, but it was enough for him to understand exactly why his sister had dropped everything to bring this to him.

"It's not April Fool's, is it?"

He honestly couldn't believe what he was seeing. Their parents had bought a lake cabin in the Cascade

Mountains when he was a little kid, and they'd spent every summer there until Rafe was fourteen. That was when their father had lost his job, and everything had changed for their family. It had sucked when they lost the lake house, but it had been far worse to watch their father lose his self-confidence and turn gray almost overnight. Worse still, they'd still been grieving over the unexpected loss of their father's brother, Uncle Jack. It had been a difficult time for the West Coast Sullivans and, even now, Rafe didn't like to think back to those years.

"As soon as I saw this listing, I rescheduled my appointments to race over here to show it to you."

Rafe glanced down at the flyer again. It didn't look as if a single thing had changed since he'd last been there, and he was glad to see it. Man, he'd loved that place— had looked forward to summer all year long because of it. Hiking, swimming, boating, fishing, waterskiing... and girls. So many pretty girls in bikinis—it had made a teenage boy's head swim.

"You've got to make an offer," Mia insisted. "Today."

He could practically smell the campfires, could feel the cool water cover him as he jumped off the end of the dock. But he'd already been over this with himself a hundred times. He had employees who counted on him. He had half the Seattle elite banging on his door, demanding he investigate their spouses. He wasn't a kid anymore with no responsibilities. He couldn't just pick up and leave his business behind.

Rafe forced himself to put the paper down on the table in front of him. "My next client will be here in fifteen minutes."

"Have Ben take her for you."

"Ben has his own appointments."

"He's good with your screwed-over wives. Better than you, actually, because he's less cynical about it all."

Rafe was six foot three, with broad shoulders and big hands. People rarely called him on his bullshit. But though his little sister was a foot shorter and weighed at least sixty pounds less, she wasn't the least bit afraid of going toe-to-toe with him.

"We can all see what this job is doing to you," she told him now. "Seriously, you should have seen the way you looked when I walked in. Heck, look at yourself right now—you're stressed out just *thinking* about meeting with another client."

His sister was a know-it-all. The problem was, sometimes she actually did know what she was talking about. Still, he had to say, "You think it's that easy? That I can just buy the cabin, turn over my clients to Ben and head out for the summer?"

"Why can't you? I mean, you *are* the boss."

"You're the boss over at Sullivan Realty, but you're not exactly buying a lake house and leaving your employees to pick up the slack."

"True," she agreed a little too readily, "but there's one big difference between you and me. I like my job. Besides, when's the last time you took a real vacation?" Before he could reply, she said, "Fact is, there are always going to be people cheating, so there is always going to be more work coming your way. You're the only one who can press the pause button, Rafe. Especially after what happened to you with—"

His glare cut her off before she could talk about the same damn thing that everyone had been talking about for the past couple of months—the knife wound to the side of his ribs. He was over it. Why couldn't they be? The guy had barely hooked the tip into Rafe's skin before Rafe had thrown him across the parking garage.

And yet it grated more than he liked to admit that his little sister was right about his taking some time off. Not because he was afraid of being jumped again in a dark parking lot, but because a guy needed to recharge his batteries every once in a while. Sex was usually good for that, but lately even the few hot hours in the sack he'd managed with women who weren't looking for love any more than he was had fallen pretty damned short of the mark.

Mia was also right about his employees; he'd made it a point to hire the best, and he could trust them to keep things running for a little while.

Just the thought of waking up to the sound of water lapping on the shore instead of traffic outside his window, and getting out in his fishing boat rather than handing tissues to sobbing women, had him feeling almost ten years younger.

"Okay, you've sold me on a vacation," he told his already gloating sister, "but I can rent a place."

She picked up the flyer from the coffee table. "Remember how we used to have cannonball contests off the dock and the Jansens next door would vote for the winner?" He had to laugh at the memory, the sound rusty after being out of use for so long. He hadn't seen little Brooke Jansen or her grandparents in more than fifteen years, but he hadn't forgotten them.

Rafe looked down at the picture of the lake house. "I loved this place. We all did."

Mia's gaze was no longer challenging or gloating. He and his siblings often fought and teased, but at the core of it all they loved each other…and they always looked out for each other, too.

"You loved it more than anyone, Rafe. You've got the money. It's time to finally use some of it. I really wish you'd take my advice and go clear your head out on the lake."

Rafe figured he could keep arguing with her, but what was the point? He wanted the cabin, and not just for himself. For his whole family—especially his parents, who should never have lost it in the first place. This time, he would make sure they would never lose it again.

He picked up the listing and looked more closely at the picture. At first glance it hadn't looked too different from the way he remembered it, but now he noticed the peeling paint, the overgrown shrubs, the worn and crooked front steps.

"After all these years, it'll probably need some work."

"I'm sure it will, but you're nearly as handy as Adam. And you know he'll be thrilled to weigh in on how to best fix any problems you might find. The listing agent and I have been playing phone tag all morning, so I'll find out more specifics right away. The flyer says it's furnished, so hopefully there will be enough there to get you started."

If it were any other house, he would have had Mia show him more pictures and give him the inspector's report, but he knew this place inside and out. Sure, he didn't know anything about the people who had lived in it for the past eighteen years, but how much could there be to fix?

"You win. I'll make an offer."

Mia's grin lit up her pretty face. "I knew it!"

He looked at his watch. "I've got to take another couple of clients this morning, but I can probably come over to your office later this afternoon to sign everything."

"No need." She reached into her bag again and pulled out a large folder. "Sign here, here, here and here. I already called with your initial offer so that you can snap it up before someone else gets it. Once I send this in, we should be good to go."

Clearly he needed a vacation, because he should have seen this coming. Mia Sullivan always got what she wanted.

Especially when she was trying to help someone she loved.

"One day you're going to find a guy you can't wrap around your finger," he told her as he took the pen she handed him and signed next to all the yellow flags. She was smiling when she took the papers back, but her grin suddenly looked a little forced.

He put a hand on her arm. "Everything okay, sis?"

"Everything's great." He wasn't sure he believed her, but she was already walking to the door saying, "You should be the proud owner of the lake house by tonight."

He'd seen the dollar figure listed on the offer and hadn't blinked an eye, but now he had to ask, "Just how good is my offer?"

The twinkle was back in her eyes as she said, "Good enough to hop on your Ducati tomorrow and be there to light a fire on the beach and lie back to look up at the stars by nightfall."

"Thanks, Mia." She had been, and always would be, a major pain in the rear. But he wouldn't trade his sister for anyone else.

She didn't turn back again, simply waved at him over

her shoulder. Noting that every last one of his male employees was drooling over her as she walked out of the building, his voice was harder than it would otherwise have been. "Mandatory company meeting at lunch."

With that, he walked back into his office to prepare for his next meeting…and, with a summer at the lake in his sights, to get started on writing up a revised list of duties for his staff at Sullivan Investigations.

Two

Some days, Brooke Jansen loved her job.

Every day, actually. Especially since she'd moved from Boston to live at the lake full-time and start her own chocolate truffle business. She even loved it on days like today, when she couldn't quite get her latest truffle recipe to taste just right.

She'd spent the past eight hours working on a new summer-themed box of truffles, one she hoped would please people as much as the winter-themed box she'd debuted at Christmas. Now it was time to work out some of the kinks in her back with a swim. Plus, she tended to have some of her biggest epiphanies while underwater. She had been swimming like a fish from the day her grandfather had plucked her out of her father's arms and plopped her into the lake despite his son's protests that she wasn't ready yet.

Brooke took her saucepans and glass bowls over to the sink. As she quickly washed them out she marveled at the view of the lake and the Douglas firs in the mountains beyond the water. Even though she'd been living on Lake Wenatchee for the past three years, she still could hardly believe how beautiful it was.

She'd spent every summer as a young child traveling from Boston to Washington State to visit her grandparents, Frank and Judy. She'd loved every second she'd spent outside on the sandy beach, swimming in the cool lake water, roasting marshmallows by the campfire... and spending time with the two warmest, most loving people she'd ever known.

In all those summers, her parents had only come to visit the lake house a handful of times, and each visit had been awkward, borderline uncomfortable. Mostly because her parents and grandparents hadn't seen eye to eye on much of anything...especially her. Her mother and father weren't ogres by any stretch of the imagination, but they had always been so focused on their careers that they often seemed to forget they had a child who wanted to have fun. And when they had focused on her, she'd often sensed their disappointment that she was neither cuttingly sharp like her lawyer mother, nor brilliant like her economist father.

They'd wanted a little baby Einstein. Instead, they'd gotten Strawberry Shortcake.

On top of that, it had been so difficult for her mother to get—and stay—pregnant with her that from the moment Brooke was born, her parents had treated her like a terribly fragile glass sculpture. All her life, they'd been afraid of her getting hurt, even though Brooke had been the most careful, conscientious child and teenager around for miles. Well, apart from that one night when she'd snuck out of the house like every sixteen-year-old on the planet and made a mistake they'd never let her forget...

Brooke was twenty-three years old when her grandparents died, their car skidding out on a patch of ice on a remote mountain pass. Though three years had passed, the hole in her heart was as big as ever. They had willed their summer cabin to her, obviously knowing her parents had no interest in it, along with the full contents of their bank account.

She'd been so devastated by their sudden deaths that, after the funeral, her parents had tried to convince her that it would make more sense to go back home to Boston and then return later, when she was stronger, to go through their things. But when she'd gotten to the departure gate at the airport, instead of getting on the airplane, she'd kissed her stunned parents goodbye before turning around and leaving the terminal.

Everything in her grandparents' lakefront home was just as they'd left it. She'd stumbled into the house and barely made it to her grandmother's favorite rocking chair in the living room before her legs gave out. *How could they be gone?*

Her grandmother's recipe book had been on the coffee table, and she'd picked it up with shaking hands. Her grandfather had made the wooden cover engraved with a heart surrounding their initials in his wood shop, a gift of love for the wife he'd adored from the first moment he'd set eyes on her. There was a large crack down through the center of the wooden heart—the result of age and being dropped once too often.

When Brooke opened the book, on top of the first recipe she'd found a picture of herself and her grandmother standing together at the kitchen counter, both of them wearing flowery aprons and huge smiles. Their hands were covered in chocolate, and shavings dusted the counters all around them.

Brooke had been at her happiest each summer making truffles with her grandmother. Judy's hobby was making chocolates, allowing her to share her love with friends and family. As she'd stared at the photo, Brooke realized why she hadn't been able to get on the plane with her parents and go back to her human resources job in Boston: life was too short and far too precious to waste. At that moment Brooke finally knew exactly what she was supposed to do with her life—stay here at the lake, in her grandparents' house, and make chocolates.

Her first year had been a rather daunting crash course, not only in learning the art of artisanal chocolate making, but also in how to start and run her own business. Her parents had been horrified when they'd learned she was leaving a lucrative career path to do something so risky with "so little upside." In a way their lack of support just made her want to succeed all the more. Fortunately, several small stores in town had been willing to carry her gorgeous handmade delights. Before the cushion of her grandparents' inheritance came anywhere close to running out, Brooke was in business.

Moving to the lake and starting her own company, doing what she and her grandmother loved, had been like following a faint ray of light, but she'd always known it would grow bigger and brighter every day. That's what her grandparents had taught her—to believe in herself and others, no matter what. The whole community had helped her succeed, which only proved they had been right.

After cleaning up the kitchen, Brooke walked into

her bedroom, stripped off her jeans and T-shirt, and slipped on her bikini. It had been a daring purchase that had sat unworn in her dresser until the house next door became vacant and she could be certain that no one would see her wearing it. She was just heading out to the front porch when her phone rang. When she looked at the caller ID and saw her mother's number her gut tightened for a split second before she picked it up.

"Hi, Mom, thanks for calling me back."

"Darling," her mother said, "it's always so nice to hear your voice. I just wish you didn't live so far away. Your father and I worry about you. Is everything all right?"

When, Brooke wondered, would her parents stop worrying about her? Especially since she'd only ever done one wild, stupid thing in her entire life…and that had been a decade ago.

"Everything's fine. It's great, actually." She had some fairly big news to give them and hoped they'd respond well to it. "Did I ever mention to you that Dad's colleague, Cord Delacorte, came out to the lake to visit me a short while back?"

"Oh, Brooke," her mother said in an extremely concerned voice, "please tell me you aren't dating him. He's a brilliant businessman, but from the rumors we heard during his visiting professorship a few years ago, he's *exactly* the kind of man you should be staying away from."

I'm not sixteen anymore, she wanted to shout.

Instead, Brooke told her mother, "Don't worry, Cord and I aren't dating. In fact, he's happily married."

Besides, didn't her mother realize that men like him never looked Brooke's way? She was too cute. Too

sweet. A good girl through and through, especially
after her one attempt at being bad had gone so horribly wrong.

Quickly, she explained that Cord had been given a
box of her chocolates as a Christmas gift. He'd enjoyed
them so much that he'd driven the two and a half hours
from Seattle to Lake Wenatchee to make her a business proposition. He'd talked to her about expanding the
reach of her chocolate business beyond her local area,
starting with a small boutique storefront in Seattle that
he'd oversee. If that went well—and he seemed very
confident that it would—he wanted to look toward further expansion into other large cities. He even wanted to
start a mail-order side of the business. Just this morning she'd signed the partnership papers.

"Why didn't you tell us about this before now?" her
mother asked. "I would have liked to look over your
partnership agreement before you signed anything."

Brooke's gut tightened just a little more. "Don't
worry, I found a great lawyer here and we went over
the agreement carefully several times."

Her mother was silent for a long moment. "Well,
at least Cord isn't a stranger, and I know your father
thinks very highly of his business acumen." Brooke
heard someone speak to her mother in the background,
likely one of her half dozen legal aides. "I'm sorry,
honey, but I've got to go now. I'll give your father the
news. I'm sure he'll want to discuss it with you, as well."

Brooke sighed as she hung up the phone, more thankful than ever that she had a lake to jump into to clear
her head. She loved her parents, but they could be a tad
overbearing, even from across the country. One day
soon, she hoped they'd finally realize she was all grown

up, her big mistake was well behind her now and she was more than capable of making good decisions on her own. It was why she hadn't involved them in her new partnership plans. Not because they wouldn't have had great advice, but because she needed to prove that she could do this—and do it well—on her own.

Finally moving out to her covered front porch, she breathed in the sweet-smelling air, scented by fir trees. She didn't bother to wrap a towel around her bikini-clad body as she headed down to the dock in front of her house. She'd always been on the curvier side—a sharp contrast to her slim and willowy mother—and as she'd hit her mid-twenties, though her weight hadn't gone up more than a half dozen pounds, her curves had become much more pronounced.

Brooke walked across the short stretch of grass and was nearly at the sandy shore when she heard a truck come up the driveway next door. From where she was standing, she could see a man get out and put a sold sign up in front of the house.

Wait a minute—hadn't the house only gone up for sale a day or two ago? Sure, it was on a perfect stretch of sandy beach, but it still seemed like the sale had happened at warp speed. More than that, though, even after all these years, she simply couldn't imagine anyone but the Sullivans living there.

The Wild Sullivans was what her parents had christened them, utterly appalled by the behavior of the family next door. Oh, how Brooke had secretly longed to be as wild, and as free, as they were. She had also, if she was being completely honest with herself, had more than a couple of moments of longing for parents as warm as Mr. and Mrs. Sullivan. Her grandparents were full of hugs and smiles for her, but her parents were more inclined to praise a good grade than applaud a perfect cannonball off the dock. Heck, they probably didn't even know what a cannonball was, whereas Max and Claudia Sullivan had been out there going head-to-head with their own kids in the competition. It still made her laugh to think of that day when she and her grandparents had been roped into being the judges.

And she still remembered who'd won the contest: Rafe Sullivan.

Brook had had the world's biggest crush on him. Even at eight years old, she'd been able to recognize pure male beauty in the fourteen-year-old. His three brothers were also good-looking, as was their sister and her friend, Mia, but Rafe had been special. He'd laughed louder and had been more willing to take a risk than his siblings.

Rafe Sullivan had been the most carefree—the most wonderfully wild—person she'd ever known.

The truck's tires peeling out of the gravel driveway pulled her from her musings. She hadn't seen the Sullivans in more than fifteen years. One summer they'd been there, the next they'd been gone and a boring older couple had taken their place. No more cannonballs off the dock, no more bonfires with her friends next door, no more hikes into the mountains around the lake where they pretended to be adventuring professors like Indiana Jones. The past few years, the house had been used as a vacation rental. Most of the temporary tenants had been perfectly fine, but none stayed long enough for her to become friends with them, and the final tenants had been horrible. Loud, obnoxious and more intent on partying than enjoying the lake. She'd been glad to see the for sale sign go up. Hopefully, she'd end up with another family next door that truly appreciated all the lake had to offer.

It was late enough now that the sun was about to set, and if she didn't get into the lake soon, it would be too cold for her to stay in for very long. In typical Pacific Northwest fashion, there was a slightly cool breeze in the air despite the fact that it had been a warm, sunny day.

She loved being in the water so much that she grinned even as the cold shock had her moving into a fast breaststroke intended to get her heart pumping and her body temperature up. Within seconds, she was lost to everything but the glorious sensation of swimming through the clean, clear water. A fish swam beneath her, and she felt as if she was in heaven.

She'd swum past half a dozen docks when she suddenly realized what the problem was with her latest recipe. She'd been planning to call her new chocolate collection Summer's Pleasures, but given a little time away from her kitchen she finally saw that she was being too literal.

Wasn't part of the joy of summer remembering how cold winter had been? Using that idea she thought just the slightest hint of that coolness—a pinch of mint, maybe?—would be the ideal way to highlight the lavender she'd chosen as the perfect taste of summer.

Swimming even faster now, she turned back toward her house. She couldn't wait to try out her new idea to see if it worked. When she reached her dock, she grabbed hold of the wooden ladder on the side and quickly climbed out. Slicking her long hair back out of her eyes, she hurried to get back to her kitchen and was nearly at the front porch when she heard another loud engine pull up behind the cabin next door.

A lone man had just ridden up on his motorcycle, the ends of his dark hair whipping out from beneath his helmet.

Now, that, thought Brooke with immediate female appreciation, *is what wild and free looks like.*

Her parents had taught her it wasn't polite to stare, but she couldn't remember why that admonition mattered as she watched the man pull off his helmet and run a large hand through his hair. She couldn't see his face, but she didn't need to see his features to know just how good-looking he was. His shoulders were incredibly broad, and even from a distance she could see how big—and how capable—his hands were where he gripped the handlebars.

She was so busy reeling from the blast of pure lust for the stranger as he stepped away from his motorcycle that it took her a moment to realize he wasn't a stranger at all.

Three

"Rafe?" His name came out as little more than a stunned whisper. "Is that really you?"

Her question was loud enough that he heard her and turned to face her. But, instead of responding, he didn't say a word, didn't even move.

All he did was stare, but it was okay because she was busy staring right back.

People often said memories made things sweeter than they actually were. But Brooke now knew that wasn't true at all. She had not exaggerated Rafe Sullivan's good looks over the years. If anything, her recollections had sorely underplayed just how gorgeous he truly was.

His hair was just a little too long, his skin was tanned, his jaw was dark with stubble, and he was so big and tall that she knew she'd have to stand on her tippy-toes and wrap her arms around his neck to kiss him.

The thought of doing something like that had her body instantly going warm all over despite the cool breeze on her wet skin. She'd been little more than a child the first time she remembered setting eyes on Rafe, but even then he'd stood out from the rest of his siblings as being more fun. More daring. And infinitely more beautiful.

When he still didn't say anything, she took a step in his direction. "It's me, Rafe. Brooke Jansen. Remember?"

Finally, the intensity of his dark gaze shifted into one of recognition. "Little Brooke," he said in a low voice that rippled over her, "how could I forget you?"

She had spent far too many years squashing her wild impulses. But following a wild impulse wasn't what sent her straight into the arms of her favorite Sullivan without a second thought. It was pure happiness at finally seeing him again.

He caught her against his chest as she hugged him tight. He smelled so good and the bare patch of skin above his T-shirt was so warm despite the cool evening air that she couldn't resist burying her face against him. As she held on tight, she felt safer than she had in years. She'd lost too many of her favorite people from childhood, and was infinitely grateful to be given the precious gift of having one of them back in her life.

She might have held on to him like that forever if it hadn't been for her sudden realization of just how good his hard, heated muscles felt against her cold, wet, nearly bare skin.

The little girl inside her had thrown herself into his arms…but it was the woman she'd become who wanted to move even closer.

When she was eight years old, the crush she'd had on Rafe was sweet. Innocent. But what she was feeling now was decidedly not sweet.

Nor was it anywhere close to innocent.

Wild. The thought—no, it was more desire and pure

need than it was a cognizant thought—came at her in an instant: *I want to be wild with Rafe Sullivan.*

But they hadn't seen each other in more than fifteen years—more than enough time for him to have a wife and family or, at the very least, a girlfriend he adored. When Brooke made herself step back from him she belatedly remembered she was just wearing her bathing suit. A very wet bikini she hadn't thought anyone would see her in. One that had just soaked the front of his jacket and pants.

She would have tried to cover herself up with her hands if she'd thought it would do any good, but even though she could hardly get her brain to function properly again standing this close to Rafe Sullivan, she knew there was no point.

The bikini was too small, and her curves were too big.

Flustered, all she could think to say was, "I got you all wet."

Rafe didn't look down at his clothes, nor did his gaze travel below her chin. "How's the water?"

She loved the fact that even though they hadn't seen each other in years, he asked her the question as though it was just another great day on the lake.

"Amazing." Suddenly, it occurred to her that the sold sign had been put up just before Rafe arrived. Hope lit within her. "Please tell me you just bought your old house back."

"Mia's a real estate broker in Seattle. She saw it come up on her listings." He stared at Brooke with dark eyes that warmed her even as the air continued to cool. "I didn't expect to see you still here after all these years."

"I moved to the lake full-time a few years ago."

"To live with your grandparents?"

Just that quickly, her smile fell. "No." She wrapped her arms around herself. "They passed away a few years ago." Her voice shook as she told him, "A car accident."

"Brooke, I'm so sorry. Judy and Frank were two truly great people."

His arms came back around her, and she could have soaked up his heat, his strength, forever. Instead, she made herself shift away again to stand on her own two feet. "I was just thinking how it didn't seem right that there weren't any Sullivans next door and then, just like magic, you appeared. You must be dying to get inside your place. I haven't been in it since it became a vacation rental. When the for sale sign went up, I snuck over and peeked in the windows to see if it still looked the same, but they were all covered so I couldn't see much."

He raised an eyebrow, and from what she could read in his dark eyes he seemed amused by what she'd just admitted. "Sneaking around? Peeking in windows? That doesn't sound like the sweet little girl I knew."

She shot him what she hoped was a saucy grin, even though she'd never been anything close to saucy at any point in her life. "I'm not a little girl anymore."

"No," he said in that low voice that made her hot and cold all over at the same time, "you're definitely not."

Despite the fact that he wasn't ogling her, the intensity of his gaze had her shivering and the breath catching in her lungs. She'd dated several nice men since college—safe, steady men her parents had wholly approved of—but none of them had ever made her feel like this. Especially with nothing more than a few simple words.

Wild.

The word echoed again in her head as Rafe said, "Come inside with me and we can check the place out, see how it looks."

She briefly considered heading back over to her house to put something on over her bathing suit, but since she'd already been talking with him in nothing but her bikini for this long, it would be silly to start acting all self-conscious and proper now. Especially when he wasn't exactly jumping her, or anything. Besides, wasn't this what the lake had always been about? Running around in bathing suits all day and only throwing on a well-worn pair of jeans and a faded sweatshirt when it grew too cold at night to ignore the chill.

"I'd love to," she said, and then they were walking side by side toward his front door.

Running his hand down the door, he said, "Needs a new paint job," more to himself than to her. "Mia said the key should be hidden under a rock by the entrance."

Brooke scanned the porch with him but didn't see anything that looked like a hiding place for a key. She was about to step off the porch to check the grass in front of the house when Rafe pulled something shiny out of his pocket and wiggled it in the old lock.

A moment later the door was open.

She stared at him in surprise. "Did you just pick that lock?"

"Trick of the trade."

Before she could ask him exactly what trade that was, and if it started with *th* and ended with *ief* by any chance, they both got their first glimpse at the inside of his lake home.

Brooke gasped in dismay as Rafe stepped over what looked to be the bones of a dead animal. He clicked the light switch, but no lights came on. Probably because the bulbs had either been shattered or ripped out of their sockets.

"What the hell happened in here?"

Brooke couldn't blame him for his harsh reaction. The old furniture was stained and torn apart. The rugs had holes chewed through them, and she was pretty sure there were a couple of animal nests in the corner.

"Maybe it just needs a good cleaning," she said, trying to see the bright side of things like she normally did. But even she could hear how hollow her words were. "I can help you with it." They walked through the living room and headed into the kitchen. "I'm sure it wouldn't take us long at all to—"

Her words fell away as she saw that not only were all the appliances in the kitchen gone, but several of the cabinets had also been ripped clean out of the wall. When had all this happened? During the final renter's parties that had gone on late into the night the previous summer?

In silence, they moved from room to room. The bedrooms were, thankfully, empty, although one did have a broken window. Both bathrooms were too disgusting to enter.

"Who could have done this to such a great house?" Rafe said, frustration and more than a little anger underlying every word.

She wanted to pull him out of the house and into her arms, wished she could think of something to say that would make it all better. "Stay with me, Rafe, while you fix this place up."

When his dark gaze landed on her again and held, she momentarily forgot all about his messed-up house. The way he was looking at her, his gaze finally dropping from her face to her breasts, and then lower still, made her mind go blank, her hands become numb… and her body warm up all over.

It wasn't until he said, "You don't need me in the way for however long it takes to fix up this dump," that her brain clicked back into gear. He wasn't just a superhot guy she couldn't stop drooling over. He was her friend.

And she would do anything for a friend.

"I'm right next door, and I've got two empty bedrooms. It doesn't make sense for you to go anywhere else—or to contemplate staying here," she added with a shiver of distaste at the mere thought of bunking down on the filthy floor or on one of the ratty couches.

Though what she'd offered made perfect sense, he still seemed to be warring with himself. Finally, he nodded. "I really appreciate this, Brooke. The only picture on the listing was of the front of the house, but Mia and I didn't think that mattered because we already knew it so well." He ran a hand through his hair, leaving it even more sexily ruffled than it had been before.

"I honestly think most of the renters were okay, except for the final ones," she told him. "But I never imagined they'd done this during their parties." Realizing she wasn't helping any by going on and on about it, she said, "How about I make us both a really great dinner? Remember how my grandmother used to say there was nothing homemade pasta or chocolate couldn't fix?" Even though she knew better, he looked so upset about

the state of his house that she couldn't stop herself from
adding, "Maybe it will all look better in the morning."

"Dinner sounds great," he said as he finally moved
his gaze from her to scan the interior of the house once
more, "but I'm not holding out much hope for the rest
of it."

More than ever, she wanted to put her arms around
him. In some ways—his good looks, the wild way he'd
blown back into town on his motorcycle—he was just
the same as when they were kids. But in other ways—
the intense way he looked at her, along with the faint
lines around his mouth that she had a feeling hadn't
come from smiling—he was different.

She held out her hand. "Let's get out of here."

He looked down at her hand for a long moment before taking it. His fingers were warm and strong as
they wrapped around hers. And that was when she put
a name to another one of the big changes in Rafe: *dangerous*.

As a boy, he'd been wild.

Now, he was both wild *and* dangerous.

The combination thrilled every inch of her as they
walked outside hand in hand, though she could feel the
tension radiating from him. He closed his front door. He
didn't have the key to lock it, but it didn't matter. There
was nothing inside that anyone would want to steal.

When they reached her porch, she let go of his hand
to grab a towel and wrap it around herself, tucking the
end in under one arm. As soon as she was covered up,
Rafe seemed to relax a little bit. She opened her own
door and stepped aside to let him in.

"It's good to see that your place looks just like it
used to."

"I thought I was going to need to update things, but once I moved in I realized it was just perfect the way it was." With anyone else she might have felt bad that her lake house had come through the years scar-free when his clearly hadn't, but she knew Rafe wouldn't wish his misfortune on anyone else.

Moving quickly into the kitchen, she reached into the fridge and pulled out a beer. "Any chance this will help to drown your lake house sorrows?"

"That depends. How many bottles have you got in there?"

She laughed and admitted, "Probably not enough."

When she handed it to him and their fingertips brushed against each other, she was no longer surprised when another rush of warmth moved through her. As a young girl, she'd always had a strong reaction to Rafe. Now that she was a woman, it made perfect sense that her reaction was just as strong...and that it felt nothing like a childhood crush anymore.

"I should probably throw some clothes on." And yet instead of heading into her bedroom to get changed out of her suit, now that they were standing in the full light of her kitchen, she couldn't stop staring at the most beautiful man in the world. One who, she'd noted, wasn't wearing a wedding ring.

She was standing close enough to reach out and put her hands on either side of his jaw, which was liberally dusted with dark stubble. Close enough to lean in to kiss him, too. She was shocked by a crystal-clear vision of Rafe yanking her bikini off and dropping it onto her kitchen floor while she lay naked across her counter and he did deliciously dangerous things to every inch of her body.

Brooke teetered right there, on the edge between giving him a kiss and running to her bedroom. In the end, though, she could all but taste him on her lips, a lifetime of choosing safe over wild had her taking a step back.

Four

Jesus Christ, when had Brooke turned into Marilyn Monroe?

Twenty years ago she'd been a cute kid. But now? Hell, now she was every single one of his dirtiest fantasies come to life.

Rafe pushed away from the kitchen island and moved to the window. It was a thousand times smarter to focus on the stunning scenery—and the fact that the lake house he'd just spent a boatload of money on was a total freakin' mess—rather than the stunning woman currently in her bedroom down the hall stripping off the little triangles of fabric barely covering her lush breasts and hips. Yet even as he took in the pinks and oranges of the setting sun in the sky over the lake, a sunset even more beautiful than he'd remembered from his childhood, all it did was make him think about Brooke again…and how she was also a thousand times more beautiful than he'd ever thought she could be.

He'd done some pretty stupid things in his life. Sleeping with that ex-client, for instance. But it would be a thousand times stupider to sleep with the girl next door.

Especially one as sweet and innocent as he suspected Brooke to be, even as an adult.

And really stupid now when he needed to stay with her because his own house would be completely uninhabitable for at least a week.

She'd been a pretty little girl, but six years had been a big age difference when he was fourteen and she was eight. She'd been digging with plastic shovels in the sand with Mia while he'd been out causing trouble with his brothers.

What a difference eighteen years made. One hell of a difference. She had a set of curves that had made him practically swallow his tongue when he'd looked at her and realized who she was. He could see the cute little girl she'd been in the pure sweetness of her smile and in her big, guileless green eyes. For all their physical beauty, the women he was used to dealing with always seemed to look older than their years. Whereas Brooke, whom he seriously doubted had even a fraction of the financial advantages of his clients, looked happy and lighthearted.

He couldn't screw around with her. Of course they'd be friends like they'd always been, but he wouldn't make the mistake of letting himself touch her again... even if she had the softest skin he could ever remember feeling beneath his fingertips.

Fact was, staying this close to temptation was a bad idea. A really, really bad one. But he couldn't figure out a way to explain the potential perils of their situation without making her think he was the world's biggest d-bag. Which was exactly what he'd sound like if he said, *I'm afraid I'm going to lose control and convince you to do dirty things with me that you'll hate me for in the morning.*

He could only imagine the way her pretty expression would fill with disgust as she wondered exactly what those dirty things were....

He was so focused on trying to force his lust-filled visions away that he didn't hear her come back into the room until she said, "You must be starved after riding here from Seattle." She'd changed out of her supersexy bikini into dark leggings and a hip-length long-sleeved shirt that should have made it easier to forget how gorgeous she was, but only made a guy wonder more about the soft skin just beneath the fabric.

For years he'd watched women calculate their worth, offer themselves to the highest bidder and then wonder why it all went wrong with the CEO they'd snared. It was second nature for him to assume that Brooke knew exactly what she was doing to him.

But nothing about the way she'd behaved since that first moment spoke of calculation. She hadn't faked the pleasure in her eyes at seeing him again, nor had she thrown herself into his arms to try to turn him on... even if that's exactly what had happened. And clearly, she hadn't worn the little string bikini for his benefit, either, since she couldn't have known he'd show up at the lake tonight.

As she walked into the kitchen and took out a battered recipe book that he vaguely remembered as belonging to her grandmother, he offered, "What can I help with?"

She waved him over to the bar stool on the other side of her kitchen island. "Finishing your beer."

Rafe couldn't remember the last time he'd been so

comfortable and so on edge at the same time with a woman. Of course, the edge was only there because he was a pig who couldn't turn off his libido for three seconds around an old friend.

He took a seat at the kitchen counter and finally noticed the big stainless steel bowls drying by the sink. "What are those for?"

"Chocolate." She smiled at him, a beautiful smile that did nearly as many strange things to his insides as her curves did. "I make truffles for a living."

"You and your grandmother were always making chocolate," he remembered, hating the way the light in her eyes dulled when he brought up her grandparents.

"It was her favorite hobby. Mine, too," she said with a small smile as she clearly worked to push away her grief. She ran her fingertips over the homemade wood cover on the old recipe book. "My grandfather made this for my grandmother by hand and he even etched their initials in this heart on the front. I've been meaning to take it somewhere to see if I can get this crack fixed, but I haven't wanted to actually let it out of my sight for long enough to let anyone touch it." She opened the book and showed him a truffle recipe in her grandmother's handwriting. "After my grandparents passed away, I decided to move here and turn her dream into a reality for both of us. Every day, as I'm making my truffles, I think about the daily ritual we had of eating one perfect piece of homemade chocolate." Her eyes grew even softer. "That initial taste of it on my tongue. The slow melt that felt like it was awakening my entire body. The decadent, sumptuous taste that lingered."

Just hearing Brooke talk about eating chocolate was the most sensual experience of his life. As she turned to pull eggs out of the fridge and flour from a nearby cupboard to make the pasta she'd promised him a short while earlier, Rafe had to work like crazy to get his body and his brain to obey his order to back the hell off.

"What—" He had to clear the lust from his throat. "What were you doing before and where?"

"Human resources in Boston."

He thought about that for a second and decided that, while human resources should have been a good fit with Brooke's naturally cheerful disposition, he couldn't see her in an office building wearing a tailored suit. Her laughter would have been stifled by four walls and forced air.

"You can only imagine how thrilled my parents were when I decided to chuck my climb up the corporate ladder for a career making truffles. Evidently, they didn't even send me to an expensive college to learn to make candy for a living," she said with a laugh before leaning forward as if she had a secret to share. "They don't even like chocolate. Can you believe it?"

All he'd have to do was lean in a couple of inches, and he could kiss her. Just press his lips to hers to see if she tasted as good as she looked.

"That's crazy," he said, but he wasn't talking about her parents not eating sugar. No, he was reminding himself that kissing the incredibly sweet girl next door was nuts.

"You like it, don't you?" Her voice now held a husky tone that reverberated right to his groin.

Idiot that he was, he couldn't make himself look away from her big green eyes. "Like what?"

As her full lips parted again, he nearly lost hold of his control when she said, "Chocolate."

Knowing he'd give away his lust if he spoke again, he nodded instead.

Unfortunately, when she smiled at him it did just what the huskiness in her voice had done. "Good. Then maybe you can be my taste tester this summer for the new recipes I'm working on."

Rafe could easily picture Brooke holding out a chocolate-covered fingertip for him to taste. Of course, in his vision she also happened to be completely naked. His mouth watered, his groin hardened further, and he had to pick up his beer and down it in one long gulp before he could answer her.

"I don't know anything about chocolate."

"Actually, it's better if you don't. There's nothing worse than an overeducated palate trying to dissect everything. I don't care about prestige or awards. All I care about is bringing people pleasure."

Just the word *pleasure* from her gorgeous mouth had him as turned on as he could ever remember being. Again it struck him that any other woman would have been doing this to arouse him on purpose. But Brooke was simply beginning to roll her pasta dough through the pasta machine, looking bright and pretty in her grandmother's kitchen.

What the hell was wrong with him, thinking anything she'd said or done so far tonight was meant to turn him on? All this time he'd thought he was better than those rich assholes he investigated, guys who thought with their dicks and screwed anything they could get their hands on. But look at him. He couldn't even be friends with a pretty girl without mentally stripping her naked.

"In fact," she said, "the best way to do a taste test is

blindfolded." Giving him a playful glance, she reached into a kitchen drawer and held up a clean kitchen towel. "This would probably work if you're game to try a few of my new chocolate recipes later tonight."

Rafe immediately shook his head. "I'm happy to try out your new recipes, but I won't wear a blindfold."

"Oh," she said as she carefully put the towel back into the drawer. "Okay."

How could he explain to her that he didn't trust anyone enough to willingly allow them take away one of his senses? Figuring it was best to change the subject at this point, he said, "Last I knew you were an eight-year-old who swam like a fish." Somehow he needed to remember to look at her as that little girl, rather than the gorgeous woman she'd become.

"And you were a fourteen-year-old boy who got into more trouble than anyone else." He was glad to see her smile come back so quickly. "I'll bet you still do."

Her question should have been light, but the idea of getting into trouble with her had his body heating up in all the places he'd been trying to cool down.

Focus. That's what being this close to Brooke was going to be about. Holding focus on anything except how pretty she was, how soft her skin looked, how sweet her mouth would taste, how surprisingly sensual it was watching her manipulate the pasta with her bare hands...

What the hell had they been talking about? Oh, yeah, what they'd been up to during the past eighteen years. Rather than answering her question about trouble, while ignoring the slight burn from the scar across his ribs that proved he hadn't yet learned how to walk away from it, he asked, "Where do you sell your chocolates? Do you have a store in town?"

She shook her head. "I supply local grocery and gift stores. But," she added with a smile that held obvious pride and excitement, "I just took on a new partner who will be opening a retail store in Seattle."

Rafe knew better than to stick his nose into someone else's personal life or business affairs unless they'd hired him to do just that—no one wanted advice they hadn't asked for—but Brooke was a friend. And he couldn't stand the thought of her being taken advantage of.

"Congratulations. What kind of things is your partner taking care of?"

"All the financial stuff," she said, as if it were no big deal that she'd turned her money over to someone else's care. "Distribution channels. Packaging. Running the retail store."

"You trust her that much?"

"Him," she clarified, before adding, "and yes, he was a colleague of my father's at Harvard, and has a great reputation in the food retail world. Why wouldn't I trust him?"

Rafe could think of a hundred possible reasons, but before he could start laying them out one by one, she began to slide the spaghetti strands into a pot of water she'd put on to boil and said, "Now that you've heard my long and winding story, tell me all about yours."

"I run a private investigation agency."

"I should have guessed that," she said with a wide smile. "Talk about the perfect job for you."

"What makes you think it's perfect for me?"

She gave him a strange look, as though she couldn't

believe he was asking her that. "Whenever we played hide-and-seek you always won, because you were able to put together clues no one else could."

"That's just a kids' game, Brooke. And you were always giggling and giving yourself away."

Her laughter—all grown up now and layered with sensuality he couldn't possibly miss—washed over him. "You haven't forgotten your nickname, have you?"

"No, but I was hoping you had."

"Not a chance, *Tracker*."

He groaned. "Remind me to strangle Mia the next time I see her for ever coming up with that."

"I'm sure no one outside your family and mine knew it," she assured him, "although no one has ever forgotten the way you found that scared little boy in the mountains."

His parents had just told them they were losing the lake house. Rafe had escaped to the mountains to try to run off the painful thought of losing the one place that truly felt like home to him. He'd found the local search-and-rescue crew trying to locate a missing boy whose family was on vacation at the lake. As far as they knew, the kid had been chasing after his dog when he left their rental house. The dog had come back home, but the boy hadn't. The crew had been afraid that the skinny five-year-old wouldn't make it through the night in his T-shirt and shorts. Young enough to run, and to keep running after as many dead ends as he needed to, Rafe had used his tracking skills to locate the little boy. Forty-five minutes later, he'd found the kid shivering with dried tear tracks on his cheeks.

"Being a P.I. in Seattle seems like the grown-up version of what you always used to do."

Rafe had spent his life watching people ignore every clue around them. But Brooke, it seemed, didn't miss a single one. Which also meant it was unlikely that she'd missed his clear attraction to her.

"Although I do have one question for you." He braced himself for her to say all the usual things people did, such as asking him about exciting stories he hadn't felt like telling for a long time. "Can you teach me to pick a lock, too?"

Feeling like it would be corrupting her to teach her something like that, he said, "You don't need to know how to do that, Brooke."

Strangely, she looked a little disappointed by his answer, but instead of pushing him on it, she asked, "How long do you think you'll be able to stay up here, away from your office?"

"A few weeks. I've got a half dozen great employees who will be running the place for me while I'm here."

She gave him an expectant look, as if she was waiting for him to tell her more about his P.I. career, but Rafe didn't feel like talking about it. He hadn't told anyone about his discontent with his career. Not his employees. Not his friends. Not even his family. He'd simply continued doing his job, even though he could no longer remember why he'd ever wanted to do it in the first place.

Fortunately, instead of asking him questions he didn't want to answer about why he hadn't gushed about his job, she said, "I was so surprised when your family sold the house. I missed you all so much."

It suddenly hit him that she must not know what had happened. "That winter after our final summer here, my father lost his job. He couldn't find another job that paid anywhere close to what he'd been making."

He didn't tell her the bank had actually taken the house…and that the stress of barely being able to keep them afloat on savings and then loans from friends had turned his father into a shadow of his former self.

"I'm sorry to hear that. I hope it wasn't too long until things turned around for your family."

"Eventually Dad got another job." At lower pay with a boss he didn't see eye to eye with. "And Ian started working while he was in college, which helped." His oldest brother had walked away from the chance to play pro football to help out their family, but Ian had done it without a word of complaint.

Brooke didn't seem surprised to hear it. "Ian was so much older, but he always made sure that the bigger kids on the beach weren't messing with me and Mia."

That was his oldest brother to a T. He took care of the people he loved—no matter the cost to himself.

"What is he doing now?"

"Ian has pretty much singlehandedly taken over the business world with his investment company. He's brilliant at picking which businesses to get behind."

"Is he in Seattle, too?"

"No, he's living in London right now."

"I so wish I hadn't fallen out of touch with all of you. What about everyone else?"

"Mom and Dad retired a ways back." Again, because Ian had pretty much forced them to. Not that they minded working in the garden and going out sailing at the club on one of Dylan's boats.

"Are they still blissfully in love?"

From the way she asked the question, Rafe could

guess that Brooke was a believer. Not only that love was possible…but that it could also last a lifetime. What would she think if he told her stories from his job about men and women who promised each other forever, and then split at the first sign of trouble?

Still, for all of his cynicism, Rafe had to admit, "They are."

She looked extremely pleased to hear it. "I can still remember the way they would walk down the beach holding hands and kiss when they thought no one was looking. And how they would sneak off to be alone while you guys were busy roasting marshmallows over the campfire. It was so romantic."

"What was romantic to you was gross to their own kids," he informed her, but he didn't disguise the affection in his voice when he spoke about his parents.

She laughed at that, but said, "I never saw my parents kiss. The only time they ever seemed truly passionate around each other was when they were debating legal cases or supply-and-demand curves. I don't think I would have minded seeing a little romance now and again. Speaking of romance," she said, before pausing for a moment in which her cheeks flushed slightly, "what about you and your siblings?" Her smile seemed a little too bright as she asked, "Are any of you married? Kids?"

"Well, Ian was married for a short while, but right now we're all wild and free."

"Wild?" She almost seemed to choke on the word.

"Mia has half the men in Seattle wrapped around her little finger, and she doesn't give a damn about any of them."

Brooke frowned. "But is she happy?"

"I think so." Although that flash of emotion in her eyes when she'd come to see him in his office the day before had made him wonder if that were true. "She's the go-to person in Seattle for swanky estates."

"I'd love to see her again."

"As soon as I tell her you're here, I'm sure she'll drop everything to come visit."

Which, he figured, would be a really good thing. Because if his sister was here, then there was no way he could accidentally slip up with Brooke by stripping her clothes off and using them to tie her to her bedposts.

"What about Adam? No, wait," she said, "let me guess. Is he an architect?"

Rafe was amazed by how perceptive she was, especially considering she'd only been a child the last time she'd seen his family. "Close. He rehabs historic homes."

She nodded as if it made perfect sense. "He was always building things when we were kids. I'd find him working with Grandpa fixing a broken pipe or putting on a new section of siding or trying to make a canoe by hand."

"Good thing he's better at fixing up houses than he is at building boats. That canoe must still be at the bottom of the lake."

"Wasn't he going steady with that girl from across the lake?"

Had Brooke had a crush on Adam when they were younger? And if she had, why did it matter? It wasn't like Rafe was going to lay claim to her, regardless of how much the caveman inside him wanted to do just that.

"He was, but that ended when we left the lake."

"All of you are so good-looking, I just don't get wh—" She seemed to realize what she was saying a beat too late, her cheeks flushing with embarrassment. "I just mean that I would think women are beating down your doors, so…" Her flush deepened. "Ugh. I should stop talking already. I'm just making it worse."

Damn, she was cute. And sexy. Who knew that would be such an irresistible combination?

He'd have thought she'd be married by now to some perfectly nice guy, with one kid holding on to her leg and another, smaller one in her arms.

Strange how easy it was to see her with those kids, and to know what a great mother she'd be. The guy, on the other hand, he couldn't quite picture. Not when he knew there weren't many guys out there who would be good enough for Brooke.

"You remember my eight cousins in San Francisco?"

She grinned. "Boy, was that a crazy week when they all came to visit. I always thought it would be amazing to have all those other kids to play with—five in yours and eight in theirs."

Rafe sometimes forgot that everyone didn't have a big family like he did. Brooke only had her parents and grandparents.

Knowing it would please her, he said, "Every last one of them is paired off now."

He'd never been with a woman he could fully trust, but he'd managed to suspend disbelief for his charmed cousins in San Francisco. Along with his parents, they were the exception. But at the same time, he couldn't understand how they'd all decided to take such a massive risk. Because if there was anything he'd learned during the past seven years, it was that even if one person wanted to be steadfast, odds were the other person wouldn't be. He sure as hell hoped his cousins could keep proving him wrong.

"All eight? That's wonderful." Just as he'd expected, she looked extremely pleased by the thought of so many happy couples in one family. "What about Dylan?" She scrunched up her nose. "Although I'm still not sure I've forgiven him for making me go sailing with him that day when the winds were at twenty knots, and he told everyone I barfed over the side of the boat."

"If it makes you feel any better, he's still taking women out on boats until they barf, which probably explains why he's still single." She was laughing as he told her, "Only difference now is that he's *building* the sailboats."

Brooke was still grinning as she drained the water from the pot and added butter, cheese and a dash of pepper to the pasta. "And on that fantastically appetizing note, dinner is finally served."

When Rafe took a bite of her pasta, he nearly groaned with pleasure. "This is damn good, Brooke."

She looked as if he'd just told her she'd won the lottery. "Thank you."

They ate in companionable silence while enjoying the sound of the frogs and the crickets outside. Finally, she pushed away her half-full plate and yawned. "Sorry. I had to get up early this morning to finish boxing some orders to deliver before the stores opened today."

"What time did you wake up?"

"Five a.m."

"I've kept you up too late. You need to go to bed." He stood and took their plates into the kitchen. "I'll take care of cleaning up."

"You rode all the way here from Seattle on your motorcycle." She moved next to him to turn on the water and start the dishes. "You must be tired, too."

His first mistake was putting his hands on her waist to pull her away from the sink.

His second was not letting go.

And his third was almost lowering his mouth to hers.

Somehow, he managed to take a step back. "Thank you for dinner. It was great." He forced himself to look away from her gorgeous face and those curves that wouldn't quit. "And thanks for giving me a place to stay. Now I'm going to wash your dishes, and you're going to bed."

Alone, damn it.

"You haven't had one of my truffles yet. Don't you want one for dessert?"

Hungry for something he knew would be a hell of a lot sweeter than chocolate, he said, "I'd love one."

"I wonder which flavor I should give you...." She licked her lips as she stared at him, and he couldn't keep his gaze from dropping to her full lower lip and then the beautiful bow at the center of her upper. "How hot do you like your spices?"

"Hot."

Her beautiful lips curved up. "I had a feeling you'd say that." From a clear plastic container on the counter she took a piece of chocolate with a red swirl across the top. "Try a bite of this one."

She didn't hand him the chocolate, but lifted it to his mouth instead. He leaned down and bit into it. Spice and steam instantly hit his tongue, followed by the smooth, rich flavor of dark chocolate.

"You like it, don't you?"

With his mouth full, he could only nod.

"Have the rest."

Her voice was husky, and though the truffle was amazing, he wanted to bite into her instead. When she moved just a little bit closer to feed him the other half of the chocolate, the sweet scent of her hair and skin had him swaying toward her just enough that his tongue slicked over the pad of her forefinger.

Her pupils dilated, and he could have sworn he heard a small gasp fall from her lips at the tiny contact.

Somehow, he convinced his feet to take a step back from her again. "Your truffles are delicious, Brooke."

"Thank you."

They stared at each other for several heated moments. "I've kept you up too late. Go to bed." *Before I do more than lick your fingertip.*

"Take either of the guest bedrooms and let me know if you need anything." She paused and looked up at him with her big green eyes. "Anything at all."

His head swam with thoughts of all the things he needed from her. Backing her up against the wall. Pinning her against him with his thighs between hers. Pulling the long-sleeved shirt over her head. Lowering his mouth to the soft swell of her breasts. Drinking in the sweet sound of her gasps and sighs as he laved her skin with his tongue. Lifting her into his arms before lowering her onto the bed. Using her shirt to tie her arms above her head to her bed frame. And then loving the hell out of her with his hands and mouth until she was begging for more. Begging for all of him.

"I'm not going to need anything." The words came out harder than they should have, but that was only because he was mere seconds from losing control entirely and acting out the scene his brain had just scripted.

"Okay." Her mouth started to move up into a smile, but fell before it got all the way there. "Good night, Rafe."

For a moment, he thought—prayed—she might turn and walk out of the room without giving him a hug good-night. But then she was moving closer and wrapping her arms around him. Of course he had to put his around her, too.

Once he was there, he couldn't do a damn thing but breathe her in...and relish every single inch of her body against his.

"Good night, Brooke."

After she finally moved out of his arms and walked down the hall to her bedroom, he finished cleaning up the kitchen. The dishes didn't take him long, but before he headed back to the small guest room, he made a quick sweep of the house. First, he checked that all the windows were latched—of course, most of them weren't—and then he checked the locks on the front door.

When they were kids, the lake was a safe place, but after working as a cop and then a P.I., Rafe no longer trusted in that safety, not even in a sleepy little town like this. He couldn't stand the thought of anything happening to Brooke living as a lone woman on a mostly deserted stretch of road off the lake. First thing tomorrow he'd pick up some better locks at the hardware store.

His ride out to the lake had been a good one, but that many hours on his motorcycle could be exhausting. Still, he knew if he got into bed now he'd only end up lying there fixated on the beautiful woman down the hall, so he started doing push-ups until he was dripping with sweat. Sit-ups were next, a hundred and then a hundred more, until his abs were burning as badly as his arms. By the time he'd finished his impromptu workout, then taken a much-needed shower and climbed into bed, he should have been burned out enough to fall asleep.

But every time he closed his eyes, he saw Brooke standing, dripping wet in her bikini, her expression at once innocent and yet innately sensual. He'd taken the small guest room farthest away from her. The double bed barely left room for a dresser and one side table but, frankly, he hadn't trusted himself to sleep with only one wall separating them. Not if it meant he could hear every time she rolled over in her bed. Not if it meant he'd be unable to stop wondering if she had changed into pajamas…or if she slept in the nude like he did.

Reeling with full-on need that he hadn't even come close to squashing, Rafe closed his eyes again and willed himself to sleep.

He'd need every ounce of focus tomorrow to keep his hands off Brooke.

Five

The next morning, Rafe woke to the sound of the shower running. Even though it was fairly cool in the house, he was sweating. He couldn't have imagined having this kind of reaction to Brooke, but that didn't change the fact that he was.

Pissed at himself, he yanked on his jeans and pulled his cell from the pocket. His sister picked up on the first ring. "How's the lake?"

"The lake is great. It's the house that's the problem."

He waited for her to exclaim with surprise, or to ask him exactly what the problem was. But all Mia said was, "When I finally got hold of the selling agent last night, she mentioned it needed a little TLC."

"TLC?" He might have laughed at that ridiculous understatement if his system hadn't been so twisted up with impossible desire for the beautiful, entirely off-limits woman in the shower down the hall. "You should have seen the look on Brooke's face when we walked in there, crunching over dead-raccoon bones."

Of course, Mia didn't comment on the animal bones,

not when her ears had perked up for a completely different reason. "Wait a minute—Brooke's still next door?"

"She moved in a few years ago after her grandparents passed away. They willed the place to her." As Mia made a sound of distress at the thought of Judy and Frank being gone, he added, "Brooke makes truffles for a living."

"Chocolate truffles?" He could practically see his sister drooling over the phone. "Sounds like the two of you got caught up last night," she said in a deceptively easy voice. One he knew better than to take at face value.

"She offered to let me stay with her until I fix up my place enough to be able to move into it. I figure it will take at least a week if I work around the clock."

"Wow, that's great that you're staying with her," his sister said in a voice heavy with suggestion.

Suggestion he was going to ignore, just as he was ignoring his own brain's suggestions for all the supersexy things he and Brooke could do together. Knowing Mia, she'd use her annoying little-sister ESP to pick up on his inappropriate thoughts over the phone, and he'd never—ever—hear the end of it.

He'd called his sister to mutter about the state of the house she'd bought with his money, not to talk about Brooke. But somehow everything kept coming back around to his beautiful new roommate no matter what he did. Turning his focus back to the house, he'd finally begun to walk Mia through its state of disrepair when his sister's phone beeped with an incoming call.

"I've got to take this call, Rafe, but don't worry, I'm not going to leave you hanging. It's really good to know

Brooke's taking care of you. Say hi to her for me and tell her I can't wait to see her."

The shower turned off at the same time his sister hung up on him. Rafe had a feeling Mia's upcoming trip to the lake was going to have far more to do with spying on her brother and her old friend than it would with helping him fix up the wreck of a house.

Knowing better than to allow his brain any time to focus on the fantasy of Brooke getting out of the shower and drying off her wet, naked skin with a towel, he quickly pulled on a T-shirt and went into the kitchen to make breakfast for them both.

There were several loaves of dough rising—when had she made those?—and all he could think was that it smelled exactly the way a home should. His mother had always made her own bread, and the familiar smell reached down into him, past all the crap that he'd dealt with these past few years, into the childlike and innocent part of him he'd thought was completely lost.

How, he wondered, could nothing more than a smell do that?

He shook his head against the crazy thoughts. By the time Brooke walked into the kitchen looking fresh and gorgeous in a tank top and shorts, he had dished up scrambled eggs and bacon and toast on the kitchen island for both of them.

"You made breakfast." She looked as pleased as if he'd bought her a diamond bracelet.

"I couldn't tell if you'd eaten when you got up to make these—" he gestured to the bread rising on the kitchen sill "—but it didn't look like you had."

"God, no, who could possibly eat that early?"

She sat on one of the stools and immediately dug into

her breakfast with a gusto he rarely saw in the women he dated. Not that he and Brooke were going to date, now or ever, of course.

After crunching through a piece of bacon, she said, "If you ever get tired of investigating bad guys, you should open a breakfast place. Promise me that once you're back in your own house, you'll still come over and make breakfast for me sometimes."

Rafe didn't put much stock in promises anymore, not when he watched people break them all day long. But he had a feeling Brooke did, and that once she made one, she would never break it. No matter what.

"I can definitely do that," he told her, and when she smiled at him, it occurred to him that she looked a little tired. Had she had trouble sleeping, too? And, if so, were her reasons anything like his?

Thank God he was going to have a long, exhausting day ahead of him getting started on cleaning up his place. Best-case scenario was that he'd work so hard and so far into the evening that all he'd have the energy to do was fall into bed…and sleep without dreaming of Brooke.

"I was thinking," she said after she'd eaten half the food on her plate, "that while you're hauling out furniture, why don't I get going on cleaning? I have a feeling that just getting rid of the layers of dust and grime on the floors and counters and walls will make a big difference."

"You're already giving me a place to stay. I can't let you drop everything to clean my disgusting house, too."

"And I can't let you deal with that place alone. Besides, I've already made the rest of my big deliveries for the week, so I can easily afford to take a day or two off."

She was still cute, not to mention sexy as hell, but also clearly stubborn enough that he knew he wasn't going to win this one. Unfortunately, a full day of being near her wasn't going to help him put the brakes on his attraction to her.

At the same time, knowing she would be there with him made the task seem less daunting.

"Thanks," he finally said. "But first I need to head out to the hardware store to pick up new locks for your doors."

She looked at her front door and then back to him with a confused frown. "What's wrong with my locks?"

"Everything."

"I almost never lock the doors anyway. No one does around here. You know that."

"Maybe this was a safe place when we were kids, but I don't want you taking any risks now."

Rafe was the one who could see through people, who, with nothing more than a look, could know their secrets and lies. But as Brooke stared at him, he felt as if she was the one looking too deeply into him.

"This is still a safe town, Rafe. Just like when we were kids."

"Just let me replace the locks on your doors, Brooke."

She thought about it for a moment before finally agreeing, "Okay."

Unfortunately, any relief he felt was countered by her honest admission: "But I'll probably forget to use them, so I don't know how much good they'll do if some crazy person shows up in town to break in and attack me."

Rafe could barely bank his fury at the thought of anything ever happening to the too-trusting woman sitting across from him. "Don't ever joke about something like that. It isn't funny."

Coming out into her kitchen and finding Rafe making breakfast had felt like a dream come true, especially when he made the best scrambled eggs she'd ever had. With his big hands and rugged handsomeness, she could only imagine the way women must throw themselves at him...and how many he must have caught over the years to take to his bed.

It felt so natural to have him in her house—two friends who had been lucky enough to reconnect after so many years apart—that Brooke had found herself questioning everything she'd felt last night. Was Rafe truly darker and more intense now? Had she invented the frustration she'd seen on his face when he'd told her, ever so briefly, about his job as a private investigator? And had she imagined the hard tone in his voice when he'd told her flat-out that he wouldn't let her blindfold him for a taste test, obviously because he didn't trust her?

Or was it simply that she'd been so surprised to see him—and had been so bowled over by his good looks— that her brain had spun off in ridiculous directions? Particularly the ones that had kept her up part of the night, dreaming of what it would be like to have his hands, his mouth, on her.

But just when she'd almost convinced herself that he was still the same carefree soul he'd once been, he'd brought up the locks and his concern that she was putting herself in danger by not dead-bolting herself inside. Even as she'd tried to tell herself it was just some guy thing, she knew it wasn't.

Her parents had taught her to obey the rules and not to ask questions that might offend someone or shake things up. But Rafe was her friend, and she cared too much about him to worry about putting herself out on a limb.

"What happened, Rafe? Why are you so concerned about how secure my house is when you know as well as I do that virtually no one locks their doors or even their cars here at the lake?"

"People do bad things everywhere, Brooke. Even here." With those parting words, he was out the door and heading off to the hardware store on his motorcycle.

He came back thirty minutes later with what had to be the biggest lock the local hardware store had in stock—an ugly silver dead bolt that looked scary all on its own—and a brand-new loaded toolbox. During his absence, Brooke had been trying to focus her attention on a second round of the new summer-with-a-hint-of-winter truffle recipe she'd been so happily working on the day before. But now, her recipe came a distant second to the beautiful enigma kneeling in front of her door, screwing in the ugly bolt.

"I'm surprised they even sell locks like that here," she murmured as she picked up the thick plastic packaging and put it in her recycling bin.

He hadn't said a word to her since he'd come back. He had simply walked in through her unlocked door and had gotten to work. Now he informed her, "I ordered some new latches for your windows. They'll be in later this week."

Brooke's natural inclination had always been to let people do what they thought was best for her. But she ended up surprising them both by pulling the screw-driver out of Rafe's hand in midair.

She took a step away from him so that he couldn't grab it back. "Why, Rafe? Tell me why you're being like this and then maybe, just maybe, I'll let you finish putting this horrible, ugly lock on my door."

He moved so slowly, so carefully toward her, that she had no doubt that he was good at his job as a P.I., and that the people he investigated never even knew he was there watching them.

"I already told you why," he said in a low voice that rumbled up her spine and made her feel hot all over.

"No," she countered, "you haven't. The last time I saw you, you were a fourteen-year-old boy who laughed all the time. You were wild and happy."

"We've both grown up, Brooke."

Even though he all but growled the words at her, instead of taking another step back as he likely intended her to do, she moved closer. Close enough to put her free hand on his face so that she could lightly stroke the stubble on his square jaw as she whispered, "Yes, we definitely have." Close enough that she could have gone up on her toes and pressed her mouth to his in the kiss she'd been dreaming of since the moment she'd seen him.

But even though she thought she read a similar desire in his eyes, before she could act on it he moved away from her…and finally started telling her what she wanted to know.

"I started on the police force after college, on the traffic beat along with the other rookies. They let me shadow a couple of detectives, and it turned out I had a knack for tracking crooks. After I solved a high-profile tech fraud case, I struck out on my own and started the agency."

"Tech fraud wouldn't have you worried about the lock on my door, though, would it?"

"Pretty early on I took on a client who was convinced her husband was cheating on her, even though she couldn't prove it. He was a very wealthy CEO of a *Fortune* 500 company and she said no one else would take on her case because they were afraid of him. She also told me that the only way she and her kids would be able to survive financially after a divorce would be if she could prove he'd cheated on her. Something about her reminded me of Mia. And I hated to think of my little sister stuck in a crappy relationship with a rich creep who held all the cards."

"He *had* been cheating on her, hadn't he?"

Rafe looked disgusted as he confirmed, "With any woman he could get his hands on."

"That's great that you helped her get out of the bad relationship."

"All of her friends felt the same way. In the past seven years, I've caught nearly every wealthy man on the West Coast with his pants down in the wrong place at the wrong time."

Being a P.I. had sounded so exciting when he'd first told her about it, but now she could see just what a difficult job it would be, if only because you'd have to constantly make a point of reminding yourself that not everyone was bad.

"That's why you're here, isn't it? To get away from the dark side of human nature for a while." When he didn't respond, she moved closer to him again and reached for his hand. Despite the fact that he stiffened at her touch, she told him, "I'm really glad Mia found you the house."

She thought about everything he'd said, everything he must have seen in the past seven years, and wanted nothing more than to erase it all for him.

"I know it's going to need a lot of work, but I think it's even more important that you have fun here." She smiled up at him, determined to see him smile back one day soon. "Who better to have fun with than an old friend?"

What the hell was Rafe supposed to say when Brooke looked up at him with those big, innocent eyes and such sweet determination to try to make him feel better about everything? It was his own twisted brain that kept spinning out into X-rated territory, not hers. By "fun" she meant swimming and hiking and roasting marshmallows over a bonfire...not licking each other all over and rolling around together on her bed until they'd both forgotten what a rotten world it could be.

Yesterday he'd been stunned by what a beauty she'd become. Today, he was surprised all over again by the way she'd grabbed the screwdriver out of his hand and demanded answers to her questions.

She was still the cute, sweet girl he'd known a decade and a half ago, but she was also a heck of a lot tougher than he'd given her credit for.

She was still holding his hand, and he wanted to tug her closer to find out if she tasted as sweet as she looked. Instead, he said, "Fun sounds good, Brooke. But I've got to know you're safe." He looked pointedly at the screwdriver.

"Thank you for answering my question," she said as

she handed the tool over without any reluctance, as good as her word despite the fact that he knew she didn't like the look of the dead bolt. "How about I head over to your house and get started with cleaning while you finish up here so that we can get to the fun stuff quicker?"

Fun. He couldn't think of the last time he'd focused on having fun. Hot sex with a stranger. The thrill of driving one of his cousin Zach's race cars. The pleasure of tasting one of his other cousin Marcus's new vintages from his Napa Valley vineyard.

But fun?

Rafe wasn't even sure what that was anymore....

"Sure," he said as he knelt back down in front of the door lock, "that sounds good."

And the truth was, just knowing he'd get to spend the day with Brooke, even if they'd likely end up spending all of it cleaning and clearing out his house next door, sounded better than it should have.

Almost like fun.

Six

They were a good team, Brooke thought several hours later as she looked around Rafe's now spotless kitchen with satisfaction. He still needed to buy new appliances, fix the flooring, and put up new cabinets and countertops, but at least you didn't need a face mask to enter the room now.

Immediately after he'd finished putting on her new lock, he'd joined her to dig into the mess the renters had made. She'd mopped and swept and scrubbed everything in her path while Rafe cleared the way for her, taking out old chairs and broken tables and linens that had holes burned into them.

She left his house only long enough to make them a plate of sandwiches and literally had to hold them beneath his nose to get him to stop working long enough to eat. Before she was even halfway through her own sandwich, he'd finished both of his and was digging into one of the dusty, beat-up cardboard boxes he'd brought down from the attic.

"I didn't think my family had left anything behind

when we moved out," he told her, "but look what I just found."

It was a frame with a faded picture in it. "Oh, Rafe, this is great!"

His whole family was in the picture, and all of them were smiling, clearly happy to be at the lake for another summer. Of course, she immediately zoomed in on Rafe. There was that easy smile she remembered and the carefree way he held his tall, lanky frame… Quite different to the way his big, strong muscles fairly vibrated with tension now.

"And there you are, just like you always were."

The warmth in his voice had Brooke turning her gaze to his face instead of back to the picture. "I'm in the picture, too?" She quickly looked down again and realized what she'd missed the first time. All the Sullivans were there, but so was she, tucked in between Rafe and Mia, smaller than everyone else, but beaming up at the camera because she'd been with her favorite people.

"I don't remember sneaking into your family photo."

"You didn't sneak into the photo, Brooke, you belonged there."

It was the nicest thing he could have said to her, even nicer than his earlier compliment about her truffles. All she'd wanted her whole life, it seemed, was to belong. Her grandparents—and the Sullivans—had made it easy for her in all the ways her own parents hadn't known how to.

Feeling as if he was holding her heart in his hand, she said, "How about I take this next door and clean up the frame?"

"That would be great." A moment later, he was heading up into the attic again.

She looked down at the photo and realized her grandfather must have taken the picture. Did he know back then what a big crush she had on Rafe? Or that it would only grow bigger and stronger over the years?

As she walked outside and across the grass to her house, the reflection of the sun off the glass in the frame momentarily blinded her so that she had to look away from it and out at the blue water and green mountains. For the thousandth time since she'd moved back to the lake, she was stunned by the beauty all around her. She hoped she never took it for granted, that she would take the time to appreciate it every single day.

It wasn't right that Rafe had been at the lake almost twenty-four hours without having been in the water. But if she suggested a swim right now she knew he'd never go for it. He was totally focused on the job at hand. Between carrying out heavy furniture by himself and crawling under the house to see how far the damage extended, it was clear he was planning on working until he dropped.

From the moment she'd seen him get off his motorcycle, he'd been too serious, too intense. Now that he'd talked to her about his job, she understood more of the reasons behind that. But the fact was that instead of fishing or hiking or relaxing on the beach, he was killing himself trying to clean up his disaster of a house. She wanted to see him smile more, laugh more, like he used to when they were kids.

A little work was fine and dandy; Brooke knew the worth of focus and determination firsthand as a small-business owner. But as she worked to wipe the frame clean, then propped it up on the kitchen counter, she figured there was nothing to lose in trying to convince him to see the wisdom of her suggestion that they have some fun together while he was there.

Knowing she'd have to be a little sneaky about it, she went back outside to the patch of grass between their properties and called, "Rafe, there's something you've got to see outside."

She expected to see his head poke out from the open—and still dirty—attic window. Instead, she heard footsteps on the roof and realized he was standing, rather precariously she thought, on top of his house.

"What's wrong?"

See, that was just it. He immediately assumed the worst about things. Was it all because of his job? Or had something else happened to give him this darker view of life?

"It's out on the end of the dock. Come quick, but be careful getting down from there."

Seeing the concern on his face, she felt a little bad for messing with him, but it was for his own good. Besides, he'd know soon enough that everything was fine. She walked out to the end of his dock and waited for him. He swung down off the roof, his long legs quickly crossing over the grass and the sand between them.

"What's the problem?"

She couldn't find the words to answer him for a long moment. Not when sweat had made his thin T-shirt stick to his chest. She'd seen pictures of men with perfect abs, but had never been this close to one. So close that she could reach out and touch him...

"Brooke?" He all but waved his hands in front of her eyes to pull her attention back to his face. "You said I needed to come down here to see something. What's going on?"

"This."

Before he could figure out her intent, she shoved him into the lake, clothes, shoes and all. The utter surprise on his face had her giggling, right before she jumped in, too.

Rafe was shaking the hair out of his eyes like a wet dog by the time she surfaced. Eighteen years ago, she would have been certain he would have thought what she'd just done was funny. But now? Honestly, she was a little nervous that he'd be angry with her, especially when she couldn't read his expression at all.

"When you were eight," he began in a deep voice that had her shivering from more than the temperature of the water, "I would have let you get away with that." He paused, and she was holding her breath until she finally saw the way he was trying to keep the corners of his mouth from twitching up into a smile. "But you're not a little girl anymore. Which means I don't have to play fair."

A second later he was reaching out to try to dunk her, but she was fast enough to swim out of reach before he could. Both of them were laughing now as he continued to chase her, and she managed time and time again to elude him. The water felt deliciously cool as she ducked beneath the surface and shimmied playfully around Rafe's legs.

She hadn't had this much fun in a very long time.

Oh, how she loved hearing him laugh, especially when the rumble of his joy danced across the surface of the water, the first real laughter she'd heard from him since last night. And, in the end, that was what sank her—she was paying more attention to the pleasure of finally making him happy for a few minutes, rather than working to make sure she stayed out of his clutches.

With one strong arm, he caught her around the waist, and when she lost her footing on the bottom of the lake because they'd gone out deeper than she'd intended, she instinctively wrapped her arms and legs around him to keep from going under.

In the space between heartbeats, playful fun shifted to heated desire.

Their wet bodies were so close that she could feel his heart pounding against hers. His fingers were flexing on her hips where he was gripping her tightly to him. She was breathing hard from their game of underwater tag, and her breasts were pushing against his hard chest. Her nipples beaded more from their close proximity than from the temperature of the water, and she could feel every hard line of his tendons flexing, every cord of his muscles…along with the thick ridge of his erection as it rose up between them.

A shudder ran through her at the sweet realization that he wanted her as much as she wanted him, and it was pure instinct to rock her hips into his. As the natural movement of the water in the light breeze brought them even closer, his name was a gasp of pleasure on her lips at the same time a groan emerged from his.

Her cheek was pressed against his, and she could hear the harsh rush of his breath in her ear even as he said, *"Brooke."*

Her name on his lips was full of enough raw passion and heat to keep her warm all winter long. She rubbed her cheek against his, and as her warm breath skittered over his earlobe, this time he was the one shuddering.

Everything suddenly made sense, that the crush she'd

had as a little girl would only mature over the years, even though they'd spent those years apart.

She'd always cared about him as a friend. Now she wanted him, too, the way a woman wants a man.

But before she could press her lips to his skin, he was unwrapping her arms from around his neck and saying in a stiff voice, "I shouldn't have grabbed you like that. Forgive me."

She couldn't understand what had happened, how he'd been hard and hot against her one second and in the next he was leaving her to tread water all by herself as he walked out of the lake and onto the shore.

For her entire life, Brooke had lived by rules of *do*s and *do not*s—rules that were supposed to keep her safe, especially after her one stupid mistake in high school. But she was tired of worrying about getting hurt by making the wrong choice. Especially when every cell in her body told her Rafe was finally the *right* one.

"Rafe, stop!"

Brooke waded through the water to the shore as fast as she could, not knowing if he'd actually stop, or how long he'd wait for her. Just because she'd decided what—and who she wanted, didn't mean that she had the first clue of how to go about getting it. It was one thing to mull all of this over in her head, but it was another entirely to do something about it.

Something *wild*.

Seven

Rafe knew he shouldn't stop, and that he definitely shouldn't turn around and drink in the vision of Brooke standing on the beach, soaking wet from the lake. But she was his friend, so he couldn't just disappear on her and pretend that nothing had happened.

Damn it, it was just his luck that she was even more gorgeous in her wet tank top and cutoff jeans than any woman had a right to be. The way she'd looked in her bikini the night before had blown him away, but with the thin fabric clinging to her breasts and outlining the lace and silk of her bra beneath, it was taking every last ounce of his willpower not to pull her back into his arms to finish what they'd started.

"Why did you just pull away?"

Instead of answering her question, he hit her with one of his own. "Why do you keep asking so many questions?"

He thought he saw her flinch, but instead of turning tail and running, she said, "Because I haven't asked any for so long. Too long. I've done what I thought I was supposed to do. I haven't talked out of turn. Or asked for anything I didn't already know I could have. I've been the good girl. The sweet girl. The *cute* girl." She tried to sneer the word *cute,* but even that was gorgeous on her. He was so fixated on her full, soft lips that he realized too late that she'd moved even closer, all gorgeous, dripping curves and irresistible woman. "I don't want to be afraid to ask for what I want anymore." She took another step closer before adding, "Especially not when I now know you want it, too."

Brooke had just singlehandedly turned what would have been a shitty day into a good one not only by offering him a place to stay and pitching in on cleanup, but by dragging him away from the work, too, to play in the lake.

And how was he thinking of repaying her?

With orgasms.

It didn't matter that she was all but begging for those orgasms. He was still acting like just as much of a pig as the guys he'd investigated. No wonder none of them could keep it in their pants. All it must have taken was a woman like Brooke looking at them with big, hungry eyes and they were goners.

Every second since he'd seen her again the night before had confused the hell out of him. He'd always known the difference between right and wrong, even as a kid. It was why he'd become a cop in the first place—to keep wrong from winning over right.

Forcefully reminding himself that tangling up with innocent, sweet Brooke in any kind of sexual way was wrong, he said, "You're great, Brooke, but we're friends."

"Friends who want each other," she countered, her gaze steadily holding his own. "I had a huge crush on you when we were kids, and seeing you again has made me realize it isn't a crush anymore."

Wow, that was a whole hell of a lot more blunt than he'd thought Brooke would be. Then again, hadn't he already learned that her soft exterior was just the packaging for determination and focus? Somehow, he needed to grab hold of the reins of this conversation—and make sure nothing more happened than one shockingly hot hug in the water.

"I'm staying with you. And even after I move out, I'll be right next door. It would be way too complicated if we pushed past being friends."

Instead of accepting his perfect logic that messing around with each other would only lead to even messier complications, she smiled at him, the surprising hint of wickedness in her eyes reminding him in the most potent of ways what every inch of her against him had felt like. The curves of her hips in his hands, her legs wrapped around his waist...and how mind-blowingly good it had been to hold her like that.

"Look," she said in a reasonable tone, "I get what you're saying—that if one of us wants out, it could be awkward being in such close proximity. But I think trying to fight the obvious attraction between us would be even weirder and would only end up causing more tension between us. We're not kids anymore. We're both adults who know how to manage expectations and hurt feelings. We're both single. And..." She paused deliberately. "We both want each other. And just in case you're worried that I'm looking for a husband and kids right now, I'm not. I feel like I've been settled forever already. Now all I want is to have some fun. And be wild. With you."

Caught between what he wanted—sweet Lord, he'd never wanted anyone as much as he wanted her—and what he knew was the right thing to do, Rafe made himself say, "If it's fun you're looking for, if you really want to be wild, we can find other ways of doing that. If you've never been on a motorcycle, I'll take you out on mine." It would be hell to have her breasts and thighs pressed against him during the ride, but he'd find a way to deal with it.

Her cheeks were already flushed from their impromptu swim, but now that he'd offered to take her out on his bike in lieu of sleeping with her, they suddenly flushed an even deeper rose. "Wow. A ride on your bike. I proposition you, and that's what you're offering me instead?" She swallowed hard, looking embarrassed suddenly by how open she'd been with him. "When we were in the water just now, and last night, even this morning, I thought you wanted me. But if you don't, then maybe we can both just pretend this whole conversation never happened."

Jesus, he couldn't stand for her to think he didn't want her, that she wasn't the most desirable woman he'd ever seen in his life. "Of course I want you, Brooke. Who the hell in their right mind wouldn't? I've been fighting with myself every single second since I saw you in your bikini last night to not reach out and touch you and make you mine."

She blinked up at him, her clear pleasure at his words mingling now with confusion. "Then if you want me so bad—and you know I want you just as much—why are you fighting so hard not to take me?"

Damn it, he'd wanted to stick with the next-door-neighbor excuse. With the it's-less-complicated-if-we-just-stay-friends line. She wasn't holding his screwdriver hostage anymore, but when someone was brave enough to call you on your bullshit, you had to have the balls to give her a straight answer.

"Last night, you called me wild. You're right. I am."

He let that sink in for a moment, let her realize he wasn't just talking about riding motorcycles and jumping off rope swings into the lake. He was talking about sex. Raw, make-her-blush-down-to-her-brightly-painted-toes sex.

"I've already told you, wild is exactly what I want."

Trying to make her understand, he said, "I promise you wouldn't like the things I want to do to you."

When a new flash of interest flared even hotter in her eyes, he suddenly realized he'd just said exactly the wrong thing. Before he could take it back, she asked, "You mean kinky things?"

Even hearing the word *kinky* fall from her sweet lips had him on the verge of losing it.

The purely honest answer would have been yes. But he'd already been stupid enough to say the wrong thing once. More than once, probably, since everything with Brooke was getting more and more mixed up in his head by the second. He couldn't live with himself if he dirtied her up. She deserved the white picket fence and the perfect guy who worked a normal job and came home with nothing heavier on his mind than whether his cousin Ryan's baseball team, the San Francisco Hawks, was going to win the World Series again.

The truth he didn't want to admit to himself, or to her, was that there was nothing more he wanted than to be kinky with Brooke. God, even thinking about what it would be like to watch the pure and raw reaction in her eyes as he pushed her to the very edge of pleasure, and then beyond—past where she thought she could go—made him harder than he'd ever been in his life.

But the fact that she was his friend—and that she was beloved by his parents and siblings, as well—made it way too risky.

If it all went wrong, none of them would ever forgive him. And Rafe would never forgive himself. Not when he knew from the start that he didn't have a damn thing to give her...and would only end up hurting her in the end.

"So I guess that means you don't think I can handle being blindfolded or tied up or calling you sir."

"I don't want you to call me sir!" He hoped she didn't notice that he hadn't said anything about blindfolding or tying her up. The truth was that right this second, those two things were at the very top of his one-handed fantasies list.

"Good," she said. "Because even though it might be kind of hot in the moment, I'm thinking it would also be a little weird."

"It's not going to be hot or weird, because you and I are not going to be anything more than friends!"

The roar of his voice echoed back at him off the surface of the lake. Jesus, he needed to get a grip, needed to somehow figure out how to turn this boat in the direction it should have been sailing all along, rather than standing there reeling at the things Brooke was saying to him.

But before he could, she was asking, "What makes you think you know what the other guys I've been with have been like? How do you know none of them have been kinky?"

Clearly, she wasn't going to let him off the hook without an honest answer...something he couldn't help but respect after dealing with cheaters and liars for the past seven years. "I know because you can hardly say the word without blushing."

"And *you* can't say the word *kinky* at all," she pointed out in that too-calm voice. "So, obviously, what we can or can't say doesn't mean much of anything, does it?"

"Brooke," he tried again, "I think we've gotten off track here. You know I care about you."

"I care about you, too."

"I couldn't live with myself if I hurt you in any way."

He expected her to finally understand and agree that they shouldn't go down this road. Instead, for the first time since they'd begun this crazy discussion, she looked hurt by what he'd said.

"Do I really seem that weak? That soft? That naïve? So innocent, so pathetic, that you really think you can hurt me that easily?"

"I never thought you were weak," he argued. "And you could never be pathetic."

"But the rest of it stands, doesn't it?"

Damn it, over the past fifteen minutes the uncharted waters he'd been trying to steer out of had only gotten deeper. "I don't know a lot of people who are soft, Brooke. Or who have managed to hold on to any kind of innocence at all. I don't want to be the person who changes you."

"It's hard to believe that in all the years I've known you, I never realized just how arrogant you are. Do you really think you could have so much power over me? Or that you could be solely responsible for changing who I am?"

Her chest was rising and falling and, for the first time, she wasn't smiling. Instead, she was glaring at him while he worked like hell not to notice the way her wet tank top was stretching tight across her incredible breasts.

"I don't—"

She cut him off. "You've been lucky enough to be wild your whole life. Well, it's *my* turn now. I thought it would be amazing to be wild with you, but if you're not interested—or just too plain scared—then I'll have to find some other guy to be wild with."

She was moving past him now, clearly furious. Rafe knew he should let her go, let her cool off. Hell, both of them needed to cool off. But the thought of Brooke searching for—and finding—some other guy to be "wild" with had him seeing red.

He grabbed her arm and spun her around to face him. The sand was uneven, and he tugged her hard enough that she fell into him, her chest pressing into his, her chin still lifted for battle as she glared up at him.

"You're not finding another guy to be wild with."

"And just how do you plan to stop me? Especially since you've already told me you're not going to tie me to your bed."

A man could only be pushed so far…and that final taunt pushed Rafe a thousand miles past his limit.

His mouth came down on hers, hard and demanding. She met him just as fiercely, her tongue tangling with his, her lips sucking while he bit at hers, then biting him when he was the one sucking in her soft, sweet flesh. One of her hands was caught between their chests where he was holding her wrist, while the other tangled in his hair as if she was trying to pull his mouth even closer.

She tasted faintly of chocolate, but mostly of pure, sensual woman. He'd been trying to convince himself that she was still just the little girl next door, but it was a woman he held in his arms. One with dangerously seductive curves and hollows that his mouth was perilously close to exploring after he'd had his fill of her lips.

"You taste so good," she whispered when he finally managed to drag himself away from her mouth.

He couldn't lie to her, couldn't pretend he didn't want her more than he'd ever wanted another woman in his life. Especially when they were so close that he knew she could feel every inch of his desire against her stomach.

"So do you, Brooke. So damned sweet."

She lifted her head and the softly sensual look in her eyes nearly undid him the rest of the way. "Then forget all of your excuses, all of your reasons, and come to bed. Taste more of me. *All* of me."

He couldn't help but reach out to trace the contours of her beautiful face with his fingertips. She trembled against him as he gently touched her incredibly soft skin. He had always been dominant in bed, but the reins had slipped from his hands the second he saw her standing there dripping wet in her bikini.

If this summer fling—one he clearly didn't have a chance in hell of resisting—was going to have any chance of working, he'd need to work on his control.

"I've known you too long and I respect you too much to treat you like some girl I picked up at a bar."

When disappointment clouded her beautiful features, he hated seeing it so much that he did the only thing he could think of to make it go away. Their second kiss was even sweeter than the first, and this time he remembered to savor her more, to slow himself down and start learning the curves and crevasses of her gorgeous mouth.

Pure pleasure whipped through him as he ran his tongue over her full lower lip, then drew it in between his teeth. The little sounds she was making as his tongue slid over hers, the small tremors just beneath her skin as she pressed her wet body closer to his, had him struggling to contain the wild sensations jolting his system.

It was going to kill him not to just take her to bed right now, but even if they were just going to be friends who had sex—*wild* sex, God help him—he wouldn't be able to live with himself if he didn't at least treat her well while they were sleeping together.

"We're both going to think things through tonight, and then tomorrow night, if you still decide you want this—"

"I'm still going to want you, Rafe. Just like I want you right now."

He didn't know how the hell he kept from kissing her again, but one more little kiss would be a direct gateway to taking her right there in the sand. He needed to make sure that she had the time to think things all the way through.

"Twenty-four hours." But even as he insisted on the waiting period, he couldn't bring himself to actually stop touching her. Sliding his hand down her arm to thread his fingers through hers, he said, "And as a thank-you for letting me stay at your house, helping to clean up mine, and for finally getting me back into the lake, how about I take you for a ride into town for dinner?"

All she would have needed to do right then to push

him over the edge of reason was lean in to kiss him again. One more kiss and he would have been done for in twenty-four seconds rather than twenty-four hours.

He was more disappointed than he wanted to admit to himself when she simply nodded.

"Okay, I'll accept your invitation to dinner, but I've got to take a shower first." She gave him the most beautifully wicked smile he'd ever seen. "A really *long* shower."

On that shockingly seductive note, she slid her fingers from his and began a slow walk up to her house.

He knew exactly what she was doing, that she was purposely taunting him with visions of her touching herself in the shower while he waited to take her to dinner. He had no doubt whatsoever that sweet little Brooke Jansen was going to keep pushing him closer to the edge during every one of the next twenty-four hours, and that she'd continue to laugh and smile through each and every one of them.

And hot damn if it didn't make him want her even more, knowing that the good girl next door not only had such a well-hidden naughty streak…but also that it seemed nothing could dim the naturally bright light inside her.

Eight

Brooke dried and braided her hair before choosing a pair of skinny jeans and a blue-and-white long-sleeved striped top to wear for their motorcycle ride and night on the town. After she'd made her suggestive comment to Rafe about the shower, her legs had just about given out on the way back into the house. She'd never been so bold before, but the rush that had moved through her at his reaction was easily worth the butterflies in her stomach.

He'd looked stunned...and also like he wanted to throw her over his shoulder and drag her back to the nearest bedroom to do dirty things to her.

She had hoped a few minutes by herself would help calm her enough to make it through dinner with him. Instead, the warm water rushing over her overly sensitized skin had only heightened her need. One kiss was all it had taken to arouse her beyond reason. She was no stranger to self-pleasure, but something told her that instead of taking the edge off, touching herself would only make her crave *his* touch more.

Anticipation and heightened pleasure, she also suspected, were quite closely linked. And when she and Rafe finally came together—if the two kisses they'd shared so far had been anything to go by—it would be explosive.

She should have guessed that just kissing Rafe would be better than any other sexual experience she'd had. He'd tasted so delicious—a little salty from the hard physical work he'd been doing all day, and fresh and wet from the lake at the same time.

She was heading into the living room when her phone rang. She could see Rafe waiting for her on the front porch—hopefully wallowing in all the things she might have been doing in the shower for the past thirty minutes—and would have just let it ring until she saw her new business partner's number on the small screen.

"Hi, Cord. I'm just walking out the door for dinner."

She listened with one eye on Rafe as Cord quickly told her that he'd found the perfect Seattle storefront and had emailed her several pictures of the space. "That's great. I promise to log on and look at the photos before I go to bed tonight. I'll give you a call back in the morning." He told her they'd need to make a deposit as soon as possible, before one of the half dozen new cupcake makers in Seattle decided to snap up the space. "I'll transfer the money into your account tomorrow. That way, we're ready to jump when we need to." She felt bad about cutting the call short, but for one night, chocolate could wait. After disconnecting, she put a couple small boxes of chocolates into her bag.

Despite the fact that Rafe was staring out at a truly serene and peaceful lake view, he looked tense.

"Good shower?"

Brooke didn't bother to stifle her delighted laughter

at his rather growly question. "Amazing." She grabbed a coat and was already heading down the steps and out toward his bike when she took a deep breath, then boldly added, "But it would have been even better with you."

She didn't turn back again to see how her sexy comment affected him, but she was pretty sure she heard him stumble on the gravel. If he wanted to mess around with her by forcing a twenty-four-hour waiting period on them, then she was more than happy to mess with him right back, she thought with a wide grin.

Especially when the good girl inside her had just learned how truly satisfying it was to be bad.

Back on the beach, his desire for her had been obvious enough that she doubted it would have taken much more than stripping off her wet clothes for him to forget about the stupid waiting period and just take her. But despite how badly she'd wanted that, she also understood that while seducing Rafe was bound to be amazing, both of them as equal partners in seduction would be so much better.

She wouldn't ever regret being with him or second-guess it.

She didn't want him to regret or second-guess, either.

His motorcycle was a sleek black Ducati. She barely knew anything about motorcycles, but even she'd heard of this brand. Brooke ran an appreciative hand over the smooth, shiny finish.

Rafe reached into the saddlebag and pulled out two helmets, one big and one a little smaller. She hadn't thought about whether or not he'd have a second helmet with him, but even though she was glad he did— she wanted to be wild, but there was a big difference between wild and stupid—she couldn't help but wonder why.

"You get a little line right here—" he reached out to stroke the tip of one finger between her eyes "—when you've got a question you want to ask me."

That one little touch was all it took for her breath to go. "I'm just surprised you have a second helmet." One clearly sized for a woman.

"Mia's got a thing for my bike. When I realized I wasn't going to win the battle to keep her off of it, I bought her the helmet so she'll always be safe when I take her for a ride."

Rafe was great for so many reasons, but right at the top of the list was how much he cared about his family. A moment later, he reached out to push a lock of hair that had fallen out of her braid behind her ear, then slid the helmet onto her head and did up the chin strap for her.

At last, the grin she'd been dying to see came as he looked at her. "Damn, you're cute."

For so many years, she'd hated that word. *Cute.* But when Rafe said it, it didn't sound bad at all.

"What do I need to know?"

"Lean with me into the corners. Follow the line of my body. And promise me that whatever happens, you won't let go of me."

"I promise."

His eyes darkened for a split second before he put on his own helmet and climbed onto the motorcycle. She swung her right leg over the leather seat and when it turned out to be wider and taller than it looked, she instinctively reached for Rafe and put her arms tightly around his chest. They fit together so that her legs cradled the firm muscles of his hips and thighs and her breasts pressed tightly into his back. She loved feeling the hard and steady beat of his heart beneath her fingertips.

"Ready?"

"Never been readier," she confirmed, hoping he knew she wasn't just talking about the bike ride.

The ride into town was much too short as Rafe pulled over in front of the Italian restaurant less than ten minutes later. Brooke pulled off her helmet and shook out her hair, feeling like a new woman.

"That was amazing! No wonder Mia's in love with your motorcycle. That was easily better than sex."

"If that's the case, it sounds to me like you've been having sex with the wrong men."

She shivered at the heat—and the confidence—in his tone that told her in no uncertain terms that sex with *him* would be miles better than any ride on a motorcycle could ever be.

"Maybe," she agreed in a voice made breathless both by the ride and by the way his words had affected her, "but I think I want a motorcycle anyway."

She could tell by his expression that he didn't like that thought one bit. "You can ride with me whenever you want."

She raised an eyebrow. "You don't think I can handle one?"

"At this point, I don't think there's anything you can't handle, Brooke...but I'd rather you rode with me."

She would go absolutely anywhere he wanted to on his motorcycle. Anywhere, anytime.

"I loved riding with my arms wrapped around you,

too." As his eyes darkened even further, she had to ask, "Do you still think waiting twenty-four hours is a good idea?"

Clearly realizing he'd just trapped himself, he sighed and said, "You're planning to torture me for every last one of them, aren't you?"

She laughed. "I have a feeling you'll do a perfectly fine job of that yourself. Especially," her newly wicked streak had her adding, "when you find out about my pajamas."

"Your pajamas?" The two words came strangled out of his beautiful mouth.

"Mmm," she said with a nod as she headed for the front door of the restaurant and tried not to betray how amazed she was with herself for the things she was managing to say to him. "I don't wear any."

Brooke and the gray-haired hostess hugged hello, and then after Brooke gave her a couple of boxes of chocolate as a gift, she said, "Elise, this is Rafe Sullivan. His family used to own the house next door, and he's just bought it again. Rafe, you remember the Lombardis? They've owned this restaurant since we were kids."

"Sullivan?" Recognition registered in the woman's eyes as they narrowed. "Wait a minute, weren't you and your brothers the ones who egged our front window on July Fourth way back when?"

He grimaced. "Guilty as charged. I know my apology is coming years too late, but I'd be more than happy to wash dishes for you tonight to make up for it."

Thankfully, she only laughed, although she was looking between him and Brooke with a clear question in her eyes. And a warning, if he wasn't too far off the mark, that he should be careful not to do one damn thing to hurt the sweet woman standing beside him.

"You already made up for it by finding that little boy in the woods," Mrs. Lombardi said, and then, "Are you back for good, too?"

"For a summer vacation."

"Well, this welcome-back dinner's on the house for both of you," she said as she showed them to a table in the corner. A rather romantic table for two, Rafe thought.

Sitting close enough to Brooke that their knees touched was nothing compared to the ride into town with her soft curves wrapped around him. By the time he halfway recovered from that, they'd be getting back on his bike and heading home.

He'd assumed that, after their superhot kiss on the beach, things would be weird. Awkward. Strained. But apart from the way she kept teasing him, Brooke was her usual cheerful, sweet self. At no point had she tried to use emotional blackmail on him to get her way, like most of the other women he'd met.

Was it really possible that the two of them could have a sexy summer fling? Two friends who knew the score and wanted nothing more than to give and receive pleasure when the lights were out?

That's what this twenty-four-hour moratorium was supposed to be about: a time-out to let those initial raging impulses settle so that both of them could think things through rationally.

Rafe figured most of the mistakes he'd made with women in the past might have been averted with a little cooling-off period. Only, something told him there wasn't going to be anything cool about his evening with

Brooke…and that there was a distinct possibility his plan could backfire. Instead of taking a clearheaded step back in twenty-four hours, he was afraid he'd be shredding Brooke's clothes as he ripped them off her.

Hell, he'd already been about to do that on the beach. Especially when she'd informed him that she was determined to be "wild" this summer, with or without him. What if he did the right thing by walking away from her and then she turned around and picked up some creep to try out her newfound urges?

She was too trusting and it made Rafe sick to his stomach to think of all the things he knew, for a fact, after seven years as a P.I. and five as a cop, could happen to her.

Damn it, an hour in and he was already rationalizing how sleeping with her himself was the only way to protect her and keep her safe.

Right. Wrong. After all these years, Rafe thought he knew exactly where the lines were drawn. But Brooke had him second-guessing everything. Everything except the sure knowledge that she'd freak out if he actually tried anything remotely kinky with her.

Still, vanilla sex had never sounded so good before….

Nine

As soon as they'd ordered and Mrs. Lombardi had brought them two glasses of red wine, Rafe lifted his glass in a toast. "To old friends."

Brooke added, "And great next-door neighbors," as they clinked their glasses together.

Speaking of keeping her safe, as soon as they ordered, he had to ask about the phone call he'd overheard. "Sounds like things are progressing with your business in Seattle."

She nodded happily. "Sorry about taking the call from Cord right before we left. He'd actually been trying to get hold of me all day to let me know about the perfect space he found in the city for our store."

"How'd the two of you meet?"

"He was a colleague of my father's at Harvard Business School, visiting from Seattle a few years back. But it was more coincidence than anything that someone gave him a box of my truffles. He said I converted him to appreciating just how good chocolate could be. He came out to the lake with a business plan already written up."

Just then a slightly surly teenage girl, whom Elise introduced as her granddaughter Holly, brought them their salads. She kept looking wistfully out at the beach across from the restaurant's front window, where a bunch of teenagers were hanging out. Rafe remembered all too well what it had felt like to be sixteen years old with hormones taking hold of his brain cells and a body that was far more mature than the rest of him.

After the girl let loose a sigh and headed back to the kitchen, Rafe asked, "What about his personal life?"

Brooke paused with her fork halfway to her mouth and gave him a look that said she knew exactly what he was up to. "I thought you were here at the lake to take some time off from investigating people."

There was no point in denying that was exactly what he was doing. "I am, but I overheard you talking about transferring money to him." After what she'd said to him on the beach about everyone mistakenly thinking she was too naïve, too soft to take care of herself, he knew better than to imply that now. "I'd ask the same kinds of questions of anyone I cared about."

Thankfully, instead of getting upset with him this time, she smiled. "Has anyone ever told you how cute you are when you're being overprotective?"

"I'm pretty sure that's not the word Mia uses."

Brooke laughed. "I was teasing about this being an investigation. You can ask me anything, Rafe. Anything at all."

The way she said *anything* had his mouth going dry, and he had to reach for his glass of wine and take a big gulp.

The problem was that he wanted to know too much about her. Her first kiss. Her first boyfriend. Her first broken heart. If only so that he could track the guy down and kill him. The same went for her first lover... and all who had come after. He'd never wanted to be a woman's first before, had never thought messing around with virgins sounded particularly fun, but Brooke kept making him think—and feel—things no one else had.

She was a good girl. Wholesome. Nurturing. Sweet. She should be predictable and safe, but every time he was near her, he felt as if he was teetering on the edge of something dangerous.

At the same time that being with Brooke was refreshing because she didn't play games and said exactly what she meant, it was also terrifying. He'd never been with a good girl, had always stuck with women who knew the score. But even though Brooke had told him she just wanted a fling, he couldn't believe she really meant it.

"If we're going to wait another—" she lifted her wrist to look down at her watch "—twenty-three hours, then don't you think we should use them to talk?" She licked her lips in an unconsciously seductive way before adding, "Because once the twenty-four hours are up, I'm guessing our mouths are probably going to be busy with other things. Although," she added into his stunned silence, "I suppose we could always fill those hours talking about all the things we're going to do to each other...."

"Brooke." Her name was a warning on his lips. If she wasn't careful, she was going to find out just how wild he really was, right here in the middle of the small Italian restaurant on Main Street.

Of course she wasn't the least bit afraid of him. In fact, by the way her eyes were dancing, he knew just how much fun she was having playing with him. Hell, he could only imagine what she'd hit him with next. Probably ask him to draw a diagram of the kinkiest position he'd ever been in.

"How can you look so damned innocent and then say things like that?"

"I have never done this with anyone else," she said with perfect honesty, "but with you it feels so natural that I can't seem to help myself."

He could barely stop himself from dragging her across the table and feasting on her instead of his meal. Fortunately, Holly brought their food over right then, nearly dropping their plates onto their laps as she paid more attention to what was going on outside on the beach than her customers. Brooke thanked her sweetly anyway and then, for a few minutes, they enjoyed some of the best spaghetti with meatballs they'd had in a long time.

Mrs. Lombardi came over to their table to check on them. "What do you think of my grandmother's famous recipe?" she asked him. "Still as good as when you were kids?"

Rafe nodded. "It's fantastic."

Brooke put a hand over her heart and agreed. "Best I've ever had."

She had a little tomato sauce on the corner of her gorgeous mouth, and without thinking Rafe reached across the table with his napkin to wipe it off.

Their hostess took in their every move, of course, along with the fact that both of their ring fingers were bare. Her husband—the chef—came out briefly to say hello to Brooke and to shake Rafe's hand. When he went back into the kitchen, his wife's eyes were full of love as she watched him go.

"Jim and I met when we were children here on the lake. It will be fifty years this fall."

"How romantic," Brooke exclaimed. "Congratulations!"

The bell over the door rang as another couple walked in and Elise left to seat them. Brooke sighed, her eyes soft and full of romance. "Imagine being so in love for fifty years that you still look at each other the way they just did."

Rafe gestured to the couple in the other corner of the restaurant who had been either glaring at each other or arguing the entire time he and Brooke had been seated. "Seems easier to imagine couples like them. I'm pretty sure they're not going to make it another fifty minutes."

Brooke frowned at him. "How can you be that cynical when your parents are the definition of true love?"

"As far as I can tell," he told her, because he didn't want her to have the wrong idea about where he stood on romance and forevers, "my parents are the exception, not the rule."

"I know you've seen a lot of bad marriages because of your work, but from what you told me, I have to wonder if maybe they were people who never should have been together in the first place."

"Even if that's true," he argued, "it sure doesn't seem to make it hurt any less. My office manager has to buy more boxes of tissues for our clients than an allergist would." He shook his head as flashes of dozens of crying women ran through his head. "If that's how hard people cry when bad marriages break up, then I sure as hell never want to see what true love gone wrong looks like."

"But if it's really true love, then how can it go wrong?"

He couldn't believe how optimistic she was, so much so that she actually thought there were different kinds of love…and that if you hit on just the right one, you'd have won the forever lottery.

"Plenty of ways, Brooke. So many that I could spend the next twenty-three hours listing them all for you."

"I'd much rather you told me your definition of true love."

Of all the things he thought they'd talk about tonight, *true love* would never have made the list in a million years. "I'm a guy," he reminded her. With his thumb, he gestured out the front window at his Ducati. "I ride a motorcycle. I've never tried to define that, apart from knowing it only happens once in a blue moon."

"I wonder which I can get you to say first," she mused. "'Kinky' or 'true love.'"

She surprised another laugh out of him.

"Actually, I'd much rather hear you laugh like that again." And then she caught him off guard one more time by asking, "Try now. Just for fun. Pretend true love is real and out there for any of us to find."

For a moment he was so lost in her big green eyes that he couldn't remember what she wanted him to try.

Oh, right. Define *true love.*

His brain went blank until he thought about his parents. "Holding hands." She was silent as he thought more about it. "Laughing together." What else? "Being a unified front, especially when times get tough." The more he thought about the ways his parents had weathered their storms together, the easier it became to add to the list. "And celebrating together when things get better."

"Are you sure you've never thought about true love before?" she asked in a soft voice.

He shrugged. "I've never had anyone ask me to try before." And if they had, he would have laughed in their face. He was the one who asked the difficult questions, never the one who answered them. But when he'd tried to make a joke about it with Brooke, she hadn't let it go. Despite how sweet she looked, she would make one hell of an investigator. "Your turn now, since I'm guessing you've given it quite a bit of thought over the years."

"What girl doesn't think about *it?*" she asked, clearly teasing him about the fact that he still hadn't said the two words aloud, referring to true love as "that" and "it" instead. She toyed with the stem of her wineglass for a few moments. "True love would be passion that burned so hot you were almost afraid of the power the other person had over you, the way they could turn you inside out with a look, a touch, a kiss. It would be wanting to fall asleep every night and wake up every morning for the rest of your life in that one person's arms. Just like you said, it would be holding hands and laughing, and building a family together. And, most of all, it would mean being able to talk to each other about absolutely anything, knowing that no matter how hard it was to say the difficult things, you'd both still love each other...and that you'd find a way to work it out together. No matter what."

Mrs. Lombardi's granddaughter removed their plates and replaced them with a huge piece of tiramisu, and Rafe was glad for the distraction. He didn't think he'd ever seen anything more beautiful in his life than

Brooke talking about what true love meant to her. Which was crazy, considering he couldn't imagine having this conversation with anyone else—especially not any of the women he'd been out with over the years. Not when he was certain none of them had believed in the steadfast nature of love any more than he did.

"I've just realized true love is about one more thing," Brooke told him.

"What's that?"

She slid her fork into the tiramisu and grinned at him. "This cake."

He didn't know a damn thing about love, but the sinfully pleasured look on her face as she took a bite of the decadent cake had his mouth watering.

But not for dessert. For Brooke.

A few minutes later they were leaving a huge cash tip on the table and sneaking out before Mrs. Lombardi could make them take it back. Before Brooke put on her helmet, she pointed up at the sky.

"Look."

There was wonder in her voice, and it was pure instinct to slide his hand into hers as he looked up.

"In just a few days, there *will* be a blue moon."

They both looked at each other then, and in her eyes he saw a sudden unexpected flash of what forever might look like.

Looking as stunned as he felt, she took a step back as her helmet fell from her fingers to the ground. Forcing himself to drag his gaze from hers, he picked it up, and when he slid that lock of hair back behind her ear before slipping on the helmet, she trembled.

This time she got on behind him like a pro, and even

though it would have been a hell of a lot wiser to take her straight home and say good-night, after the way she'd reacted to their short ride to the restaurant, he decided to give her a treat by driving the long way home.

The sun had set, and the windows of the stores along the tiny Main Street were lit up, as were the cottages all along the water and in the woods. It would have been a great ride alone, but it was a thousand times better sharing it with Brooke.

Riding his motorcycle had always been a rush. A thrill. A release. Not foreplay. And definitely not romantic.

But it was all those things tonight.

When they finally pulled in behind Brooke's cottage and she took off her helmet, she was vibrating with energy. "I thought I was ready this time for how awesome that ride would be. If that gets better and better every time, I may explode from the sheer thrill of it. Thank you." She threw her arms around him, just as she had the night before when they'd been so surprised to see each other again. "Riding on your motorcycle, dinner and the company were all spectacular."

"They were," he agreed as he let himself hold her for a few seconds. She was warm and soft and he couldn't ever remember enjoying the feel of a woman more. After having her pressed up so close to him for the past thirty minutes, her legs and arms and hands holding him as tightly as she would if they were in bed together, all he could think about was sex…and wanting her to explode from the pleasure *he* could give her.

She yawned against his shoulder, and he made himself shift back. "You worked hard all day, not only on your chocolates but also on scrubbing down my house. I should let you get to bed now."

"I'd rather stay up with you."

He shook his head. "We both know what will happen if you do."

That little line came back between her eyebrows, and he had to press a kiss to it.

He felt the warm puff of breath fall from her lips at his touch just before she asked, "Tell me again why you think it's so important that we wait?"

He knew it wasn't a good idea, but he couldn't stop himself from pulling her closer. "Because I care about you. And I want to make sure you have time to think about this. I would never forgive myself if we slept together in the heat of the moment and you woke up the next morning and decided it was a mistake."

She looked up at him, her mouth just inches from his. "Are you sure I'm the one you're worried about?"

No, he wasn't sure about a damned thing anymore. Only that he needed to kiss her more than he needed to take his next breath.

Her mouth met his halfway, her lips soft and cool from their ride. She tasted like red wine and cake and a sweetness that was entirely her own. He couldn't get enough of her, couldn't remember one single reason why they weren't already in her bedroom, stripped down and having each other.

She kissed with the same innate sensuality with which she did everything else, from making truffles to splashing with him in the water to teasing him over dinner. He threaded his fingers into her soft hair and tilted her head back so that he could have full access to every corner of her mouth. He was starved for her, desperate for more even as he was taking everything he could…all the while sensing that he'd never be able to get enough of her.

He wanted so badly to do the right thing, but he was quickly coming to realize that where Brooke was concerned, he wasn't even close to being a strong enough man to follow through on it.

"Brooke—"

She pressed her fingertips to his mouth. "The only reason I'm not inviting you into my bed tonight is because I don't want *you* to think being with me is a mistake, either. Good night, Rafe." She went onto her tippy-toes to press one more soft, sweet kiss against his lips. "Sweet dreams."

As he watched her walk inside her house, the same question kept repeating in his head over and over: What the hell had he been thinking to insist on making them wait twenty-four hours to have each other?

But he knew the answer to that already. Brooke had said she could be casual about sex, but he knew better. It wasn't who she was.

And yet, did he even have a prayer of resisting her, even with all the warning bells going off?

Knowing he wouldn't be getting any more sleep tonight than he had the night before, he grabbed a couple of thick blankets from one of the chairs on the porch and headed down to the beach. Lying back with one arm under his head and the blankets thrown over him, he stared up at the stars and worked to focus on the beauty of the clear night, the sound of the light breeze rustling through the leaves, the frogs calling back and forth to each other…but his head was spinning, reeling still with the taste of Brooke and his desperate need for more of her.

Only twenty hours to go…

Ten

The next morning, Brooke wasn't surprised to wake up and find Rafe's bedroom door open and the room empty. He wasn't the kind of man who could ever be idle, especially not when he was trying to distract himself. Hopefully, she thought with a grin, he wouldn't be too exhausted at the end of their twenty-four-hour wait. Because once he was finally in her bed, she wasn't planning on letting him do much sleeping at all....

She hadn't thought she'd be able to sleep a wink with all the anticipation shooting through her veins, especially not after a good-night kiss that had completely rocked her world, but she'd ended up getting a fantastic night's sleep. Probably because she wasn't at all nervous about being with Rafe.

She was looking forward to making love with him as the best darn treat she'd ever have, better than the richest, most decadent truffle could ever be. Yes, there was a chance that he could change his mind and decide not to risk their friendship by throwing hot sex into the mix but, given the way he'd kissed her the night before—a shiver followed by a bolt of heat went through her just thinking about his kiss—she figured the odds were pretty darn low that that would happen.

She'd intended to help him with his house again today, but she'd meant what she said about not wanting to rush him into being with her, either. Something told her that the two of them together in the same house, even with brooms and hammers in their hands, would have both of them quickly forgetting all about giving each other more time to think things through. And the truth was, she did have a great deal of work to do, especially since Rafe had gotten her insides so spun up last night that she'd completely forgotten to check out the pictures of the boutique space in Seattle that Cord had emailed her.

Ten hours later, she'd not only approved the Seattle storefront and transferred the funds to her partner, she had also finally perfected her Summer's Pleasures recipe. Rafe might have distracted her from her work the night before, but today she'd felt so energized, so incredibly alive, that everything she touched had been right.

Working with chocolate had always been such a wonderfully sensual, all-senses-involved process for her, but never more than it was now. With every saucepan of heavy cream she heated up, she thought of the way his body heated hers as he pulled her close. With every stroke of her whisk through the creamy chocolate ganache, she thought of the way Rafe had stroked her skin with his big, slightly rough hands. And when she let a newly made truffle melt on her tongue, she thought of how delicious his mouth had been over hers...and how she couldn't wait to taste the rest of him, too.

Still, even as she'd worked happily in her kitchen on

her new batch of truffles all day long she'd been keeping an eye on the time.

Only one hour left, thank God.

Rafe hadn't come back to her house, but she'd seen him out the kitchen window, working even harder than he had the previous day, a look of intense focus on his face. He hadn't looked her way once, which left her free to stare all she wanted whenever he came outside.

Her mouth watered even now just thinking about how beautiful he was, the way his muscles rippled and tensed as he moved. She'd had a couple of nice men as lovers over the years, but although she had a perfectly fine time in bed with them, her world had never spun off its axis, either. Some people, she assumed, were meant to give their passions to other things. Her parents had the law and economic theory. She had chocolate, and she'd tried to be satisfied with that, even though she'd always harbored a sense there might be something more.

With nothing more than a handful of kisses, Rafe had stirred up her deeper passions in a way she hadn't believed could be possible. And Brooke now knew she'd never be satisfied with anything less.

When the clock ticked down to the final forty-five minutes, and she finally left the kitchen to go back into her bedroom to strip off her clothes, Brooke shivered at the thought of Rafe melting on her tongue the way one of her chocolates did. It wasn't hard to guess that she probably wasn't like the women Rafe normally slept with. Not only because he'd used the word *innocent* to describe her, but also because tall, dark, handsome men like him were always with the sleek, exotically beautiful female equivalent.

She didn't need to step in front of her full-length

mirror to know that she was anything but sleek and exotic. Deliberately reminding herself that Rafe had already seen her in a bikini and had clearly liked what he'd seen, she went to take a shower. She'd never been a high-maintenance woman, but tonight she shaved and then smoothed lotion on every inch of skin in heady anticipation of his touch.

Wrapping a towel around herself, she dried her hair, then opened her closet door and stared at her clothes.

What does one wear to be kinky? Especially given that her wardrobe was entirely lacking in leather and chains.

Well, she definitely didn't want to look like she was trying too hard. Good thing that wouldn't be hard to do with a wardrobe that consisted almost entirely of sundresses, shorts, jeans and tank tops. In the end, while she chose a simple white cotton dress with spaghetti straps and a fitted bodice, it was what she chose to wear under it—or *not* wear under it, to be more specific—that had her feeling truly sexy. Maybe even borderline kinky.

She couldn't wait to see how Rafe reacted when he realized that she'd left both her bra and her panties in her dresser drawer.

Because no matter what he'd said about being more than she could handle, she knew she was safe with him. Only a true friend could give her such a great gift: the chance to play with fire, knowing all the while that he'd never let her actually get burned.

She was reaching for her makeup bag when she looked into her bathroom mirror and realized that her cheeks were flushed and her eyes were already bright enough without any blush or mascara. Even her mouth was pink, as if just thinking about Rafe's kisses had been enough to give her a just-kissed look.

Five minutes left.

Her heart had been beating a little bit faster all day long. Now it pounded like crazy.

All night, all day, her brain had kept replaying his words: *"Last night, you called me wild. You're right. I am wild."* Brooke took one last look at herself, but barely saw her reflection in her rising excitement.

How had she possibly lasted twenty-four hours?

She opened her bedroom door and walked barefoot into the living room. The way the soft cotton of her dress slipped and slid over her naked curves only increased her breathlessness, especially when she realized Rafe was already there.

He turned from the window, his hair still damp from a recent shower. He smelled clean and masculine and utterly delicious and looked beyond gorgeous in his jeans and T-shirt. Even his bare feet were tanned and beautiful.

For a long moment, they stood and stared at each other across the room, just as they had two nights earlier when he'd arrived on his motorcycle and she'd just come from swimming in the lake.

Finally, Rafe broke the heady silence. "The way you look tonight. In that dress. Jesus, Brooke, you're beautiful." He seemed to lose his breath, and then they were both moving toward each other.

She didn't know who reached whom first, just that her hands were suddenly in his and he was tugging her close. Every single movement, every touch, felt so right. So perfect.

So meant to be.

"It's been twenty-four hours." He slid both hands up her arms and shoulders and neck until he was stroking her cheeks with the pads of his thumbs. "How do you feel?"

"I ache." Her confession was barely more than a whisper.

His dark eyes flashed with so much heat that the breath she was barely able to take caught in her throat.

"You ache," he repeated in a raw voice. "Where?"

"Everywhere."

On a groan, he was lowering his mouth to hers, and she could almost taste him when he stilled barely an inch from her lips. "Last chance, Brooke."

God, she could hardly think straight when she wanted to kiss him this badly, but she knew it was important that she make sense of what he'd just said. "For what?"

"To change your mind." A muscle jumped in his jaw. "Tell me to let go of you, and I won't touch you again."

Just the thought of him not touching her made her gut twist painfully. "Don't you dare let me go."

She clenched her hands in the fabric of his shirt to pull him closer, and their mouths met in a hot, almost frantic kiss. She was desperate to make up for the one thousand, four hundred and forty minutes they'd lost— she badly needed to fill in all the kisses they'd missed out on.

As if he could sense she needed soothing, he slid his hands into her hair and lifted his mouth just far enough away from hers so that their lips were barely touching. She could feel his warm breath on her damp mouth, and she shivered even as he kissed her again, more gently this time, with just the barest press of his lips against hers.

His kiss was at once sweet…and commanding. Without a word, with just the barest of touches, he was slowing them both down, letting them savor each other rather than simply devouring without thought or appreciation.

And, oh, how he savored.

No one had ever kissed her like this, taking the time to taste every last inch of her mouth, from corner to corner, from the upper bow of her top lip to the lush center of her bottom lip. Her hands opened and closed on his shirt as waves of pleasure moved through her. And then his tongue was moving back inside her mouth to find hers, causing another sweet shock of bliss to shoot all the way down to her toes. Without a bra on, her full breasts were peaking hard against the bodice of her dress, and she instinctively moved her hands from his chest to wrap them around his neck so that she could press herself into him.

That was when he lifted his head to stare down at her with such heat and more desire than she'd ever seen on a man's face. "You're amazing."

"I've never felt like this before." With anyone but Rafe, she might have been shy about expressing her desire, might have been unable to put words to her erotic feelings. But she knew she was safe with him…even as the lust that spiked inside her was the most dangerously beautiful thing she'd ever known. "I've never needed anything, *anyone*—" his teeth bit into her lobe, and she gasped with pleasure "—as much as I need you."

A moment later his mouth caught hers again. She lost

herself in his kiss, in his delicious taste, in the shockingly sensuous feel of his tongue stroking over hers.

"Tonight," he murmured heatedly against her lips, "isn't nearly long enough for all the things I want to do to you."

"You can have as long as you need," she told him, her arousal ratcheting up even higher at the thought, the question, of what those *things* might be. As he lowered his mouth to the curve of her shoulder, she couldn't wait to find out.

His teeth nipped into her skin at the exact moment he slid one slim strap down. She loved the slick of his tongue over the small bite, and then the incredible sensation of his full mouth sucking against a part of her body she would have sworn wasn't the least bit sensitive or sensual. A moment later he was giving her other shoulder the same treatment, stripping her even as he tasted her flesh with a small bite followed by the warm lash of his tongue and then a split second of suction against her skin that had her trembling in his arms.

When he lifted his head, his eyes were blazing with the same heat and need she knew must be reflected in her own.

"I need to see you," he said, his low voice rasping over her skin as if he'd touched her instead.

"Yes," she whispered. "Please."

With the utmost gentleness, he moved his hands to her bodice and slowly slid the material down over the upper swell of her breasts, just to the point where her nipples were about to show. He stopped then and looked up into her face.

"You're not wearing a bra."

"Only the dress," she confirmed for him.

His eyes widened. "Only the dress?"

She nodded and boldly reached for his hands, placing them over her hips so that he could feel the truth of her words for himself. His eyes closed and his nostrils flared as he cupped her bottom, then slowly ran his hands over her.

"So damned beautiful, Brooke."

She'd never heard anyone speak to her, about her, with such awe. But before she could tell him she thought he was beautiful, too, he was sliding his fingers through hers and tugging her toward the bedroom.

"I've already waited twenty-four of the longest hours of my life for you. I can't wait another second."

They had just walked inside the bedroom when a loud knock came at her front door. Both of them stilled and looked toward the front porch, then back at each other.

His hand tightened on hers. "Were you expecting someone?"

"No. Maybe if we ignore them they'll go away."

But, of course, the knocking sounded louder the second time. Rafe ran his free hand through his hair in clear frustration. A moment later, he was pulling Brooke's dress all the way back up and sliding the straps into place on her shoulders. He lowered his mouth to hers for one last, hard kiss that would have spiraled off into more were it not for the continued pounding out front.

"Go answer your door before they break it down."

Rafe went with her into the living room, and when she saw who was standing on her porch through the picture windows, utter shock made her temporarily mute as she opened the front door.

"Oh, my gosh." Mia Sullivan pulled a completely surprised Brooke into a warm hug on the front porch. "Look at you! You're absolutely *gorgeous,* Brooke."

Adam Sullivan's arms came around her next, the second Sullivan brother to hold her in the past fifteen minutes. When he let her go, his eyes were warm as they moved over her face, and he agreed, "Absolutely gorgeous."

The next thing she knew, Rafe was standing on the porch with the three of them, glowering at his siblings.

Eleven

Rafe couldn't believe his luck. He'd waited twenty-four goddamned hours to have Brooke naked beneath him...and *that* was when his brother and sister showed up unannounced?

It had to be some kind of sick joke, karma coming back around to kick him in the ass for every bad thing he'd ever done.

Or, he thought with a tight clenching of his gut, was it a sign that he should keep his hands off her?

Normally he would have been happy to see his sister and brother, but tonight all he wanted, right or wrong, was for them to turn around and go home to Seattle so that he could have Brooke all to himself.

"What are you doing here?"

"Surprise!" Mia said as she lifted a bottle of sparkling wine. "We came to toast your new house with cousin Marcus's finest bubbly from Napa, and to see what we can do to help you fix it up before we head back to Seattle tomorrow. Mom and Dad would have come but they're off sailing with Dylan for a couple of days. And, for all we know, Ian may never return from London."

Rafe should have been grateful for his siblings' help. Instead, all he could say was, "So you're staying the night?"

"Rafe, it's late. Of course they're staying." Brooke gestured for everyone to follow her inside with a wide smile for his brother and sister. Where she'd been so loose in his arms just moments before, now her movements seemed a little stiff. "I'm so glad you're both here. It's been way too long."

Mia and Adam weren't stupid—not even close— and they had to know something was up. It wasn't hard to put the signs together: his crankiness at their unexpected arrival combined with her just-kissed mouth, flushed skin and the fact that she was wearing the sexiest little white dress on the planet.

With nothing underneath it.

God help him.

Rafe's hands fisted as he remembered the way Adam had hugged Brooke. All Rafe had been able to think about was ripping his brother away from her and tossing him headfirst into the lake. Adam was a good guy, but he was no saint where women were concerned. And Rafe could tell just how much Adam was appreciating Brooke's exposed curves and creamy skin.

What guy with a pulse wouldn't?

"We decided it would be fun to surprise Rafe." Mia's eyes twinkled as she looked between the two of them. "And, boy, are we glad we did."

"Are you hungry?" Brooke asked.

"We ate dinner on the road," Mia replied, "but I'd love to take the bubbly outside and drink it while eating s'mores around the campfire." She lifted another bag that held graham crackers, marshmallows and chocolate.

"That's a great idea," Brooke said, still not looking at Rafe.

Was she embarrassed to have been nearly caught naked with him by his siblings? Or was it simply that she was as frustrated as he was about not being able to finish what they'd waited so damned long to start?

"Since I'm sure both of you are dying to get a look at your old house," Brooke said. "How about I meet you all out there after I change into something warmer?"

Yes, that was a good idea. Maybe if he went next door, where he couldn't see Brooke, couldn't smell her freshly soaped skin mixed with a hint of arousal, he could get his shit together enough to make it through the night.

Less than sixty seconds later, the three Sullivans were inside their old house, standing under the one flickering lightbulb hanging from the ceiling illuminating what would be the living room once he put the place back together.

"I'm glad to see things haven't changed much," Adam said. "I know there are some cosmetic problems, but it still feels like home, doesn't it?"

Though Rafe was still enormously irritated that his plans with Brooke had come to a crashing halt, Adam's clear excitement was infectious. "Can't wait to get to work on it, can you?"

"I had plans for this place even when we were kids," his house-rehabbing brother confirmed. "As soon as Mia told me you got the place, I found them and pulled them out." Adam patted his pocket. "I'll show them to you once we've settled in at the bonfire."

Throwing himself into working with Adam on plans to fix the place up was likely the only way Rafe was going to make it through another night apart from Brooke without losing it. But he already knew no amount of going over renovation plans was going to push her whispered confession about aching for him out of his head.

Working hard to pull his focus back to the house, Rafe said, "You're right that the bones of the place are good, but whoever's owned it for the past fifteen years obviously wasn't too concerned about maintenance. I was thinking—"

Mia cut him off with the loud clap of her hands over her ears. "Please, stop. I've just had to spend the last two and a half hours in the car listening to Adam's plans to renovate this house. Can we please talk about something other than support beams and load-bearing walls for a little while? Like, maybe, how totally freaking beautiful it is here?"

At their sister's urging, they turned to look out the front picture window at the moon just rising over the lake. "Still one of the greatest places in the world," Adam agreed, but he was clearly chomping at the bit to go over every square inch of the house. He grabbed the flashlight lying on the floor by the door and said, "I'll be back in a couple of minutes."

As soon as he walked away, Mia turned her gaze from the lake and pinned Rafe with it. "Are you and Brooke sleeping together?"

No, damn it, but only because you showed up at exactly the wrong time.

"It's none of your business what the two of us are or aren't doing."

Her gaze didn't waver. "You need this house, Rafe. The lake. Some time to get away from all the garbage you deal with at work." Mia's expression was far more serious than usual. "I love Brooke, and I'm thrilled she's back in our lives, but do you really think it's a good idea to get involved with her when she lives next door?"

Damn it, he hated to hear his sister echo his own concerns…especially when he'd nearly rationalized them away in the heat of unquenchable desire. "Everything's going to be fine, Mia."

A flicker of surprise crossed her eyes. "You're not going to listen to reason, are you? Although," she added before he could respond, "if you don't start dating her, given how big Adam's eyes got when she opened the door, I'm sure he'd happily step up to the plate."

"She's not going to date Adam," Rafe told her in a hard voice. "And we're not dating, either."

Mia's eyebrows went up. "Then what are the two of you doing? Because it sure didn't look like you'd been playing a friendly game of canasta when she opened the door."

"I already told you, it's none of your business."

"You're my brother. She's my friend, one I haven't seen in far too long." Mia sighed dramatically. "When you're done screwing around, I'm going to end up having to choose sides…and of course I'm going to have to choose you just because we're related."

"There aren't going to be sides."

"How can you know that for sure?"

"Brooke's an adult. So am I. Even if we have some fun together this summer, no one's going to get hurt."

"Oh, crap," his sister said on a groan. "You haven't made some kind of crazy agreement with each other to have a no-strings summer fling, have you?"

"Mia." He said her name as a warning to drop it, but of course his little sister just ignored him.

"Let me see if I can think of a time no-strings has ever worked out for anyone." Sarcasm dripped from every word as she made a show of mulling it over. "Nope, can't come up with a single one."

"Brooke's a heck of a lot tougher than you're giving her credit for."

"I'm sure she is," she said. "But has it occurred to you that maybe it's not her I'm worried about?"

Nothing his sister could have said would have surprised him more. He and his siblings might have spent most of their lives ribbing each other, but at the end of the day there was no one they cared about more than family. Clearly, Mia needed some reassurance that he wasn't at the end of his rope.

"You were right that I needed a break from the job for a while, but now that I'm back here at the lake, you can stop worrying. I would never do anything to hurt Brooke. And you and I both know she's too sweet to ever hurt me."

Mia threw her arms around him and hugged him tight, a feisty little cub who'd grown into a woman who loved with the ferocity of a lioness.

"I just keep thinking about that psycho who came after you in Seattle. You know how terrified Mom and Dad were about it, but you have to know they weren't the only ones. We all were."

"I love you, too, sis." He hugged her back hard enough to lift her small frame off the floor before setting her back on her own two feet. "Come on, let's go find Adam and get that bonfire and the s'mores started."

As Rafe and Mia got a bonfire going in the fire pit on the beach, Adam finally emerged from beneath the house, brushing cobwebs from his shoulders and hair. When Brooke walked down to the beach to join them with four champagne glasses in her hands, Rafe noticed that she had changed into jeans and a long-sleeved T-shirt. Still, even with denim on instead of the sexy-as-hell white dress, she couldn't mask her natural sensuality. Instead, the hints of bare skin and lush curves hiding behind the fabric made her allure even more potent.

Here was yet another reason it was crazy to think about being with Brooke beyond a summer fling. How could he live his life wanting to kill any guy who looked at her—even his own brother? Especially when a guy couldn't help but look, despite the fact that she wasn't purposely flaunting anything.

With a flourish, Mia popped the cork on the bottle from the Sullivan Winery, fizzy liquid bubbling over the lip onto the sand. Each of them grabbed an empty glass, and after Mia filled them, they raised them in a toast.

"To Rafe's new lake house."

"To Mia, for finding the listing before anyone else could," Brooke added.

"And to Brooke's amazing chocolate truffles," Rafe said, barely able to take his eyes off her incredible beauty long enough to turn to his sister and touch glasses.

They all toasted and drank, then found spots in the sand to stretch out.

"I *love* that you make chocolate truffles for a living," Mia told her old friend. "Your grandmother and grandfather would be so proud."

Brooke's eyes immediately dampened as she gave Mia a slightly wobbly smile. "Thank you for saying that."

"We're all so sorry that they're not here with us tonight."

Mia squeezed Brooke's hand, and after a moment of silence in which they all remembered Mr. and Mrs. Jansen, Rafe badly wanted to pull Brooke onto his lap and hold her until her grief was completely gone.

"Rafe told me all about how brilliantly both of you are doing," Brooke said to his siblings. "Monopoly always was your favorite game, wasn't it, Mia?"

Yet again, Rafe was amazed by everything Brooke had noticed when they were kids. Clearly, Mia was, too.

"Yes, it was." Mia grinned at Brooke. "And making chocolates with your grandmother was yours."

"Remember when Dylan convinced me to make a batch out of mud and you ate one on a dare?"

Mia put her hand over her stomach. "Don't remind me."

"You never could resist a dare," Adam said with a grin of his own.

Just as she always had, Brooke fit perfectly into his family. She was fun to be with. The sex was clearly going to be mind-blowing…that is, if his siblings ever left and let them get on with it. She was practically already a Sullivan. Lord knew his parents would be beside themselves with glee if he decided to have more than a summer fling and bring her home as his girlfriend.

It was perfect. So perfect that he knew better than to let himself trust it.

Not when he'd seen "perfect" blown to smithereens at least a thousand times.

And yet, even knowing that—and with Mia's voice in his head telling him how summer flings never worked out—Rafe still couldn't find the self-control to give Brooke up.

Brooke turned her focus to Adam next. "Do you work on specific kinds of houses?"

"Any house that catches my eye. The era or architect is less important to me than the feel of the place. Take your grandparents' house, for instance. It doesn't adhere to any one particular sensibility, but your grandfather not only had a great eye, he knew what he liked and didn't give a damn if it wasn't strictly Craftsman."

Though Brooke's expression softened in the firelight, Rafe still thought she seemed a little on edge. "I've always loved this house. No matter where else I was living, it was my true home. I've kept it up as best I could over the past three years, but I'm sure I'm forgetting lots of things my grandfather always did."

"Tomorrow morning, how about I take a look to see how things are holding up? Your grandfather was always so good about letting me tag along and help him when he could have done the job twice as fast without me there. It's the least I can do."

"Wow, that'd be great, Adam. Thank you."

It was irrational to be irritated with his brother for offering to help out with Brooke's place. Hell, Rafe should already have offered that himself. But he was a hell of a long way from rational thought tonight.

"Honestly," Mia said, "I still can't believe you make truffles for a living!"

Rafe let her know, "You'll be even more impressed once you taste one."

"How about I bring out a few to go with the s'mores?" Brooke offered, already standing up.

"Yes, please," Mia said with a wide grin as Adam nodded his approval of that idea, as well.

Mia was about to get up to join her friend inside, when Brooke waved her back down onto the sand. "You've only got one night here. You should spend as much of it outside by the lake as you can. I'll make sure the bedrooms and bathroom have everything ready for you while I'm in there, so don't worry if I'm a few minutes."

Rafe watched Brooke practically bolt away from the three of them and frowned. She'd been her usual friendly self with his siblings, but at the same time, he couldn't help but feel that something wasn't quite right.

Standing up, he told them, "I'll take the couch so that you can have the room I've been bunking in, Adam. You guys hang by the fire while I go grab my stuff and remake the bed for you so Brooke doesn't have to do that, too."

He needed to find Brooke and make sure everything was still okay.

Twelve

Brooke truly was thrilled to see Mia and Adam again. Still, a little voice in her head that she wasn't proud of kept asking, *Did their reunion have to be tonight?*

Normally she would have loved nothing better than to sit out by a lakeside bonfire catching up with old friends while making s'mores with a glass of bubbly in hand. But she could still feel Rafe's kisses tingling on her lips, the heat of his hard muscles searing her skin through her clothes…and the heated promise in his eyes of more pleasure than she'd ever known before.

Keeping busy was the only way she was going to make it through the evening and the following day. She stepped into the walk-in closet that held the extra sheets. She had just pulled a folded stack off the shelf when she heard footsteps, and was just about to poke her head out of the closet to see if someone needed something, when Rafe walked in and closed the door behind him.

Her heart immediately started pounding like crazy, so loudly that it took her a few seconds to register the click of the lock on the door.

"Rafe? Is everything okay?"

"That's what I came inside to ask you." He took the sheets out of her arms and put them back on the shelf. "I keep thinking about what you said to me before my brother and sister showed up."

Her breath caught in her throat as she looked up at him. Somehow she managed to get out the words, "Which part?"

He took her hands and drew her against him. "You told me you ached." He buried his face in her hair, and she let herself slide her arms around him again, exactly where she wished she'd been for the past hour. "I can't stand the thought of you feeling that way all night long."

His mouth came down over hers before she could think a straight thought, and then all she could think of was his taste, the feel of his muscles beneath her fingertips, the way his kiss melted her insides until she was clinging to him just to stay upright.

"Let me take the ache away, Brooke."

Everything inside of her was spinning so fast that she couldn't think coherently. She wanted what he was offering her so badly that she could barely force herself to remind him, "But your brother and sister are outside."

He brushed a lock of hair away from her face, his fingertips burning a trail of fire across her cheek. "I know I can't make love to you while they're here, but there are other things I *can* do, things that will make you feel a hell of a lot better. They know we're getting the guest rooms set up for them. We have a little time before they expect us to come back outside."

"I want to, so badly, but I don't know if I can—" The rest of her words fell away as she felt her cheeks flush even more than they already had.

"Tell me, sweetheart," Rafe urged.

She swallowed hard as she whispered, "I don't know if I can be quiet enough for them not to hear."

Rafe's eyes dilated even further as he slid the pad of his thumb over her lower lip. "I'll make sure no one hears."

Her body flooded with a rush of liquid heat at his promise, one she didn't know how he could possibly keep. Of course, when he cupped her face in his hands and looked at her with a question in his eyes, she couldn't do anything but nod.

He reached for the hem of her long-sleeved T-shirt, and as he quickly pulled it up and over her head, he told her, "The next time we do this, I promise I'll go so slow that you'll be begging me."

Didn't he know she was already about to start begging, just from the way he'd stopped to gaze at her in her bra?

"Every time I see you, I think I'm going to be prepared for how beautiful you are." He slipped her bra straps off her shoulders. "But I never am. Not even close."

Her breath was already coming in sharp pants of need when he reached around to undo the clasp at her spine. Just like that, her breasts were bare before him, her nipples peaking beneath the heat of his hungry gaze.

"Brooke."

Her name had barely left his lips before he was cupping her breasts in his large hands and bending down to take one sensitive peak into his mouth. She clutched at his head, her hands threading into his dark hair as he licked her nipple, then closed his teeth lightly over it. His right hand played with her left breast, stroking, caressing, teasing. And then his hand was taking over where his mouth had been, and his mouth was moving to cover her other breast.

"God, you're sweet," he murmured as he lifted his head. "I need to taste more of you. Now. I need you now."

Just his mouth and hands on her breasts had been the most sensual experience of her life. But then Rafe's hands moved to the snap and zipper of her jeans before he dropped to his knees in front of her. He had her step out of them and she thought she just might combust from nothing more than the heat of his dark gaze on her.

His thumbs slipped into the sides of her panties, and even though he'd apologized for needing to move fast tonight, the slow drag of lace against her skin nearly drove her mad. She didn't realize she was holding her breath until the tiny patch of fabric hit the floor. On a whoosh of air from her lungs she started breathing again, but when Rafe leaned forward and she felt his warm breath between her thighs, she couldn't take in enough oxygen.

Her legs were trembling like crazy, but he was holding her perfectly steady with one hand around her waist, the other caressing the side of her hip.

His dark eyes flicked up to her face. "Brooke?"

She'd never done this with any other man—stood naked before him while he knelt at her feet and asked if he could put his mouth on her. But with Rafe, there was no fear, no embarrassment, no worries. Only need…and a whispered, *"Please."*

But when Rafe leaned forward and slicked his tongue over her, she realized the ache she'd had earlier was nothing compared to the way he was making her feel now with the slow lash of his tongue, the sweet press of his fingers inside her. It was as if he knew her body better than she did herself—exactly where to stroke, precisely how to caress. Nothing existed but the two of them in this moment of perfect pleasure, and oh, how she wished she could stay in this moment just a little while longer to truly savor every delicious burst of sensation. But the way he was touching her—kissing her— felt too good…and she'd been waiting too long for him to achieve that kind of control.

Just as her inner muscles started to clench around him, she whispered *"Rafe,"* in an urgent voice. Continuing the hard thrust of his fingers inside of her while his thumb stroked over her clitoris, he quickly stood up so that he could cover her mouth with his and swallow her cries of pleasure.

Brooke bucked against his hand as her climax took over every last cell. And though her body finally settled against his after the incredible orgasm, he kept kissing her as if he couldn't get enough. He continued to stroke gently over her sensitive flesh when he finally lifted his mouth from hers.

"Better?"

She couldn't yet find her voice to tell him how good he'd made her feel, but she could reach for him to curve her fingers over the thick erection throbbing behind his jeans.

"A little better," she whispered as he pushed his hips hard into her hand, and she reached for his zipper. The last thing she expected him to do next was slide his hand from between her legs and take a step away from her.

"You don't know how badly I want you to keep doing that, but there's no way you'll be able to keep me quiet."

Brooke didn't care anymore about keeping quiet. All

she wanted to do was touch him the way he'd touched her, taste him the way he'd tasted her. She was halfway to her knees when they heard the front door creak open.

"It's not fair," she protested when he pulled her to her feet.

"Since it was my stupid idea to wait twenty-four hours, I deserve the punishment of waiting for you to touch me, too."

Before she could tell him that was utter nonsense—and that she needed his pleasure just as much as he did—he was handing her her clothes. He gave her one last, hard kiss before he grabbed the stack of clean sheets.

And left her aching for him more than ever.

Thirteen

Rafe ripped out another strip of the nasty old kitchen linoleum with both hands. Up since five that morning, he'd already cleared the old flooring out of most of the house. He should have felt satisfaction at finally making some serious headway, but his gut churned whenever he thought about what he'd done to Brooke the night before.

He'd locked her in a closet, stripped off her clothes in record time and had feasted on her...all with his siblings barely a hundred feet away. Not only had he known she was nervous about having Mia and Adam so close by, but their first time together should have been special. She was the kind of woman who deserved roses and candlelight, wooing and soft words. He'd vowed to keep control of his baser urges with her, but he hadn't been able to hold to that for five freaking seconds.

One taste of her mouth, one stroke of his hands over her naked skin, and he'd lost any hope of control.

And yet, Rafe had felt a connection with Brooke that he'd never felt with anyone else. Even in the cramped room, knowing they had to stay quiet and with no more than a handful of minutes together, every kiss she'd given him had rocked more than just his body. Every taste of her had only made him hungrier for more, for the chance to lay her down on a bed and take all the time in the world to learn her beauty, her scent, her sweetness, from head to toe.

Adam walked inside just as Rafe finished pulling out the last of the old flooring. "Boy, am I glad I went for a swim this morning. Never did like pulling up linoleum. You should have come out swimming with the rest of us. It felt really good to jump into the lake."

Rafe hadn't trusted himself around Brooke in her bikini, so he'd locked himself in the house with dirty linoleum instead. Now he took the cup of coffee his brother handed him and drank it down in one big, hot gulp.

"Can I use your truck to go pick up some new flooring and kitchen cabinets?"

"Sure. I'll go with you."

The brothers were halfway to the hardware store when Adam finally addressed the white elephant in the truck. "You were inside 'helping' Brooke for quite a while last night."

Rafe hadn't been surprised when his sister had called him on the situation last night. But his brother wasn't exactly big on talking about feelings. Of course, Rafe knew Adam wasn't talking about feelings now, either. Sex was all his brother cared about. Normally, Rafe would have agreed wholeheartedly.

But Brooke was different.

"Whatever you're going to say next," Rafe told Adam in a warning tone, "I'd be careful about it."

His brother's eyebrows went up. "In that case, I guess getting the details on just how hot she is without her—"

Rafe didn't care that Adam was behind the wheel or that he'd driven in from Seattle to help with fixing up the house. He was never going to let anyone get away with talking about Brooke like she was just some tramp he was screwing around with for a little while.

Rafe clamped his hand around Adam's throat. "I said to be careful."

His brother lifted one hand from the wheel as if it were a white flag, and Rafe slowly slid his own away from his brother's windpipe.

"Jesus, you know I like her." Adam rubbed his throat and coughed, wincing as he swallowed. "She was a cute kid and now she's—" He cut himself off before Rafe could come at him again for saying the wrong thing. "Definitely not a kid anymore." Adam paused before asking, "You sure messing around with the girl next door is a good idea?"

Rafe was anything but sure. Which was why he answered his brother's question with a question of his own: "If you were in my position, could you walk away from her?"

Adam pulled into the parking lot of the local hardware store. "There's no point in bothering to answer that. She's only ever wanted you." With that, he headed in to check through the store's selection of flooring as if his brother hadn't just been strangling him over a pretty girl five minutes earlier.

Brooke and Mia were both bent over paint cans in the living room, opening up the perfect shade of blue that Mia had brought with her. Rafe and Adam were at the hardware store, and it was the first time they'd been alone, just the girls, since Mia had arrived the night before.

"Remember that time we got into the paint in my parents' basement and drew pictures on the walls?"

Brooke laughed as she shook her head at the memory of what naughty little girls they'd once been. "I still can't believe Claudia and Max were so nice about it. Instead of yelling at us and making us clean it all up, your parents even added to our drawing and then asked my grandparents if they wanted to paint with us, too."

Brooke stirred the paint with a long wooden stick, then carefully poured it into a clean plastic tray. The two of them had always been good enough friends that Brooke was more than a little surprised that Mia hadn't brought up Rafe yet. Mia had never been the kind of person to hold things in, something Brooke had always envied about her. Envied, and was trying to emulate more and more.

Which was why she decided to break the ice by saying, "When we were friends as kids, we were never quite old enough to talk much about boys."

Out of the corner of her eye she could see Mia's brush still where she was painting the trim along the ceiling. "We didn't need to talk about it for me to know that you had a crush on Rafe."

Brooke felt a flush creep into her cheeks. But she had to do more than be brave enough to bring up Rafe with Mia, she had to follow through with the rest of the discussion…wherever it led.

She put down her roller and admitted, "My crush never went away."

Mia laid her brush down, too, and climbed halfway

down the ladder. "He obviously seems to feel the same way."

From the look on her friend's face, Brooke prompted, "But?"

Mia sighed. "I love my brother, even though I want to punch him sometimes. You've probably noticed he's changed since we were kids."

Brooke nodded. "He told me a little about the work he does as an investigator. I can't imagine how awful it must be to catch that many people cheating on their spouses."

"Wow," Mia said, "I can't believe he even told you that. He *never* talks about work. Not even with us." Her worried expression fell away, to be replaced by a wide smile. "Then again, you're not like any of the other women he's been with."

"We haven't exactly—" Brooke cut herself off as she realized they actually *had,* at least on her end, last night in the linen closet. She let out a strangled laugh. "Is this conversation as awkward for you as it is for me?"

Mia laughed and said, "The really awkward thing would be if you started giving me the dirty details."

"No," Brooke promised, "I swear I'm not going to do that. Ever."

"Not that you've asked for my blessing," Mia said, "but I want you to know that you have it. Although there is one condition. Well, two, actually."

Knowing how close Rafe and his sister were, Brooke felt her heart thudding in her chest as she asked, "What are they?"

"One," Mia said as she held up her index finger, "don't ever lie to Rafe or cheat on him. I can't think of anything that would break my brother as fast as that would."

"I would never do those things," Brooke immediately protested.

"I know that, but I wouldn't be doing my sisterly duty if I didn't say it. So don't be mad at me, okay?"

"Of course I'm not mad at you," Brooke reassured her old friend.

"Good, because the second condition has to do with your forgiving nature."

Brooke raised an eyebrow. "How so?"

"You know how guys are kind of clueless and they sometimes screw stuff up without meaning to? Especially when they get scared about things moving too fast or being too good?"

"You're the one with four older brothers, so I'm not going to doubt that you're right."

"If he screws up—"

Brooke cut Mia off. "Honestly, there's hardly anything to screw up yet."

Mia waved that off. "There will be. And if I know my brother at all, he's not going to just let himself fall merrily into happily ever after."

"Happily ever after?"

Brooke couldn't breathe quite right anymore. She and Rafe were going to have a summer fling. They were going to get a little wild together. No one was aiming for a proposal and a ring.

Or was she?

If Mia could see that she was freaking out, her friend didn't show it as she said, "He's my brother so I have to love him, no matter what he does. But you get to make a choice about loving him."

Loving him? Of all the ways she'd thought this conversation with Rafe's sister might go, she hadn't taken it anywhere near this far.

"Mia, seriously, we're just—"

"I know, it's just a summer fling. But if it ever becomes more, and Rafe starts to screw things up, all I'm asking is that you try to remember that men are idiots… and that I've never seen him look at anyone the way he looks at you."

"He—" Brooke swallowed hard. "He looks at me a certain way?"

Mia smiled and leaned in as if she had a secret to share. "He looks at you like you're going to be a heck of a lot more than just a summer fling."

Brooke was glad that she and Mia were talking, but she simply wasn't sure what to say to happily-ever-afters and more-than-summer-flings. Telling herself it wasn't fair if they only talked about her, she asked, "What about you? Anything or anyone on the horizon?"

Mia shrugged. "They're all just summer flings for me."

Brooke cocked her head. "There's never been anyone special?"

"I thought so once, but I was wrong."

The pain in her friend's voice stunned Brooke. But before she could offer comfort, Rafe and Adam pulled into the driveway behind the house. As if she'd gotten a lucky reprieve, Mia went to see the flooring they'd picked out at the hardware store. Clearly, Mia was more comfortable talking about other people's love lives than she was about her own.

"Everything going okay?" Rafe asked as he moved beside her a few minutes later.

She'd just picked up her paint roller again and was having a heck of a time trying to act as if everything was normal. Especially when she was still reeling from the conversation she'd just had with his sister.

"I don't want you to wear yourself out on my behalf."

He was standing close enough to her that she could feel his heat radiating through to her skin. "Everything's great."

Her voice came out a little on the squeaky side, but thankfully, he didn't seem to notice the higher pitch.

"I'm glad to hear it, although you do have a little paint right here."

Her eyes fluttered closed as his fingertip lightly brushed her cheek. She couldn't find her breath for a long moment, not when every word, every kiss, every caress from the night before came back to her in a sweet rush.

When she finally felt recovered enough to look at him, she nearly dropped the roller at the dark heat in his eyes.

I've never seen him look at anyone the way he looks at you.

She saw wild desire and dangerous lust in his face... but was there really something else there, too? Something that had more to do with emotion than heat?

It was one thing to sleep with Rafe, to be *wild*. But to actually have a man like him to call her own, not just for one summer, but forever?

Brooke knew the truth in her heart in an instant: She'd never wanted anything so much.

Despite her parents trying so hard to protect her for her entire life, she'd taken a few risks. Moving out to the lake full-time, for one. Starting her chocolate business. Forming a partnership with Cord to expand the business. Now she realized all of those risks were simply trials for the real thing.

For risking her heart.

She knew she should be remembering what Rafe had said to her on the beach: *"I couldn't live with myself if I hurt you in any way."* He'd said it as if he were certain that he would end up hurting her if they crossed the line of friendship to something more.

And yet, when he didn't move his finger from her face after he'd removed the paint, but cradled her jaw in his hand and began to tilt her head into the position she now knew he liked best for deep kisses, all thoughts fled but one.

I want this man.

For as long as I can have him.

Chocolate truffles didn't last forever, either, but oh, how she savored that one perfect taste. She'd do the same with Rafe—she would appreciate every precious moment with him, both in and out of his arms.

His mouth was almost on hers when Adam's voice carried to them from the back door. "Hey, Brooke, you in here?"

A muscle was jumping in Rafe's jaw when he dropped his hands and took a step away from her. By the time Adam got to the living room, Rafe was already heading out to the truck to start carrying everything inside.

"I didn't want to forget to ask—is there a way to order your chocolates online?"

"Not yet, but my partner says the new website will be up soon. For now, you can just tell me what you'd like or call me from Seattle anytime. But, hopefully, you'll be coming for visits often enough to pick them up from me personally. Rafe obviously loves having you here."

She loved the way the three of them took care of each other. One day she prayed she'd have a family of her own like this, one where the kids fought and scrapped and teased, but loved even more. She smiled up at Adam. He was gorgeous, just like his brother, but he'd never made her heart race the way Rafe always had.

"I absolutely love having the wild Sullivans back next door, too," she added.

Instead of grinning at her, Adam simply stared at her for a moment, long enough that she asked, "Do I still have paint on my cheek?"

"No, you're perfect just the way you are." She felt her eyes widen at his words, but they were nothing compared to his saying, "My brother's one hell of a lucky guy."

Before she could even begin to figure out how to react, Adam was heading out of the room to help carry in the new flooring.

The sun had begun to fall in the sky by the time they'd put down the new wood flooring in more than half of the small lake house. On top of that, Brooke and Mia had finished painting the living room and kitchen. Rafe was amazed by how much ground had been covered in the past three days, especially with the help of his siblings. He'd be out of Brooke's house a heck of a lot sooner than he'd thought.

Women had always complained that he liked his own space too much, but he hadn't even come close to getting his fill of Brooke. Maybe after they'd had sex a few times...

No, there was no point in lying to himself when he knew sleeping with her was only going to make him want more of her, not less.

Brooke was back at her house working to finish up a couple of last-minute orders when Adam told Mia, "We'd better hit the road." Rafe's brother looked around the lake house with clear satisfaction. "The place is starting to come together."

"Once the furniture is in," Mia said, "it will look even better." When Rafe groaned at the thought of having to furnish an entire house from the ground up, his sister grinned at him. "I already ordered most of the furniture you'll need. They said they'll deliver by the end of the week, so you should probably make sure the rest of the flooring is in by then. I told them my big brother deserved the very best."

That was one heck of a surprise. A really good one, given that she had saved him the pain of furniture shopping. Then again, he had a feeling he was going to be a whole heck of a lot less glad when he saw how much of his money she'd spent.

On top of helping him lay the new flooring, Adam had made notes for the handful of renovations he was planning on implementing in his spare time throughout the summer when he could get back up to the lake. Considering his brother was already overloaded by clients who wanted his magical touch on the historic homes they'd purchased, Rafe knew how big a deal this offer was.

Despite how grouchy he'd been about their abrupt appearance the night before, it meant a hell of a lot to him to have his brother and sister here, all of them working to put their old lake house back to rights. He might have been the one who'd paid for the place, but as far as he was concerned, it was as much theirs as it was his.

"Thanks, guys." He didn't say for what, but he knew he didn't have to. Not when his family had always understood all the things he didn't know how to say.

They found Brooke in her kitchen, putting the lids on a couple of large gold truffle boxes. "We're here to say goodbye for now," Mia told her, "and to thank you for putting up with all of us on absolutely no notice whatsoever."

"I know we're not family," Brooke said in a soft voice filled with emotion, "but I've always felt like we were. And I love that you came without calling first, just the way family should."

Brooke hugged both Mia and Adam, gave each of them a box of chocolates, and then they were grabbing their overnight bags and heading off to Adam's truck, leaving Rafe and Brooke alone once again, standing almost exactly where they had been twenty-four hours ago.

"Our brother has it bad for the girl next door," Adam said to his sister as they left the lake behind in the rear-view mirror.

"Of course he does," Mia replied. "Who wouldn't? I saw the way your eyes nearly popped out of your head when she opened the door last night, and then again when we went swimming this morning."

"She's gorgeous," Adam admitted, "but he's dated plenty of pretty girls before."

"She's also intelligent. Sweet. And, most important, she knew him before everything got warped by his job dealing with all of those scumbags he finds cheating."

"True, though I'm sure whatever she did with him inside while the two of us were out at the bonfire last night doesn't hurt, either."

Mia made a face. "Seriously, can we not talk about Rafe's sex life with our friend?"

"Okay," Adam readily agreed.

Too readily, Mia thought. She smacked him on the arm. Hard.

"Ow!" He lifted his left hand off the wheel to rub his tricep. "What was that for?"

"Just because you're not talking about the two of them having sex doesn't mean I don't know you're still thinking about it. Probably in play-by-play detail."

He pretended to be playing a bass guitar as he sang a parody of a bad porn soundtrack. She covered up her laughter with a sound of disgust.

"Seriously, stop it. She's your brother's almost-girlfriend. And if he doesn't manage to totally screw it up, she could be more than that someday."

"Doubt that will stop me," he told her, then pretended to play the bass guitar some more.

Men. They were all pigs. Especially her brothers.

Still, she hoped against hope that Rafe wouldn't screw things up with one of the most amazing women she'd ever known, and that Brooke could be the one to finally break through the thick wall Rafe had put around himself. Every time Mia tried to talk with him about the knife attack, he immediately shut her down. Something told her that if anyone could break down that wall and heal the inner wounds he wouldn't admit to, it was Brooke.

Unfortunately, considering that her brother hadn't even stepped up to the meaningful-relationship plate enough to admit to Mia that he and Brooke were an item, she knew better than to hold out too much hope.

Sighing, she flipped on the radio and was planning to zone out for the rest of the drive when a new song came on that had her entire body stiffening.

Adam started tapping out the beat on the steering wheel. "This is such a great so—"

She flipped the radio off just as the song was about to hit the chorus.

"Why'd you turn it off?"

"I have a migraine. The music was hurting my head."

She almost never got headaches, but Adam didn't know that, so thankfully he didn't ask why she'd had such a strong reaction to the song.

Mia'd had five years to get over it. To get over *him*. She should be able to listen to his songs, at the very least, without her stomach twisting…without being assaulted by memories she'd never forget.

Fourteen

Rafe's brother and sister were finally gone, which meant he and Brooke were finally free to rip off each other's clothes and pick up where they'd left off the night before. But he couldn't stop feeling that he'd already pushed her too far, too fast, by taking her the way he had in the linen closet. It didn't help that they hadn't had any time alone during the day to talk so that he could gauge how she was feeling...or whether she had changed her mind.

Forty-eight hours ago, he'd been certain that they should curb their attraction to preserve their friendship. Even though all they'd had so far was fifteen stolen minutes of passion, he knew it wasn't even close to being that simple anymore.

Friends. Lovers. Next-door neighbors.

Family.

Brooke was already all of those things to him.

The soft lapping of the water on the lakeshore suddenly seemed too loud as the silence drew out between them in her kitchen. Rafe was never nervous. Not when he was doing dangerous undercover work, and certainly not when he was with a woman.

But being alone in the kitchen with a beautiful girl with big green eyes had his heart thumping hard and fast in his chest.

If he were a gentleman, if he had any honor at all, he'd let her say whatever it was that had her worrying her lower lip between her teeth, and then give her space if that was what she wanted. But nothing could have stopped him from reaching for her. He simply had to hold her, had to feel her soft skin heat up beneath his fingertips, had to feel her shudder at his touch.

But, for the first time, she didn't lean into him, didn't press her cheek to his or slide her arms around his neck. He could feel her heart beating just as hard as his was.

"Your sister—"

"Likes to poke her nose in where it doesn't belong."

Brooke looked far too serious. He wanted her to smile again, wanted so badly to see her cheeks flush with pleasure before her lids fluttered shut the way they always did when he kissed her.

"She loves you," Brooke said as she gazed up at him. Her gaze was full of desire, but there was worry there, too. "I've longed to be wild for so long that when I saw you again, I lost sight of anything else. I lost sight of the fact that friends should always look out for each other. I've only been thinking about myself, about what I want. You tried a dozen different ways out on the beach to keep your distance, to explain why we shouldn't do this, but I wouldn't listen. I didn't want to listen to what you wanted because I was so busy thinking about myself."

"How many times do I have to tell you that I'm *dying* to be with you, Brooke? How many different ways do

I have to show you?" His words were hard-edged with frustration, his hands flexing on the upper curves of her hips as he pulled her closer. "Hell, I wanted you so damned bad last night that I locked you in a closet and took exactly what I wanted. I told you it was for you, that I was there to soothe your ache, but it was for me, Brooke. *Me.* Because I couldn't wait one more god-damned second to feel you, to taste you."

"I couldn't wait, either," she told him, but even as she tried to absolve him of his guilt, he knew he had plenty to make up to her.

"Our first time together shouldn't have been that fast, that rushed. Let me make it up to you."

Her breath was coming faster now, her breasts pressing sensuously against his chest as she gazed up at him. He was surprised when her mouth curved into a small smile a moment later.

"We're both being silly, aren't we, arguing over which one of us has been more selfish? Maybe," she said with a slow smile that transformed her face into a beauty that took his breath away, "we could argue, instead, over who can give the other person more pleasure tonight?"

The weight that had been pressing on his chest all day finally began to lift as he smiled down at her.

"We're not going to argue about anything at all," he said as he slid his hands down her hips to cup her soft curves. "Because tonight is going to be all about you. All about your pleasure. All about your needs."

He could feel her heartbeat speed up against his chest as she said huskily, "I like that idea. A lot. Only, last night I never did get to—"

He covered her mouth with his before she could remind him of what she'd been about to do in the linen closet. The problem was, that vision of her starting to drop to her knees in front of him had been burned into his retinas, and he'd been hard as a rock thinking about it nearly every minute since then.

He moved his hands from her hips and up over her gorgeous hourglass figure so that he could slide his fingers into her hair and tilt her head at exactly the right angle to plunder her mouth with his tongue. And then neither of them was wary anymore as their hot kiss pushed away any concerns they had about hurting each other.

Pleasure.

That was what they'd focus on tonight—the only thing that mattered.

Yesterday, there'd been plenty of time to get nervous, to plan and anticipate. But the past twenty-four hours had been so full of unexpected guests and emotions that Brooke was almost surprised to finally find herself in Rafe's arms.

As he kissed her and she melted into his arms the way she did every time his lips touched hers, she knew there had never been any reason for nerves or worries. Nothing had ever been as natural as the passion between them—two friends who had been destined to become so much more.

And it was their past—all the little connections that had been forged over summer barbecues and sand-castle contests between a young girl and a beautifully wild teenage boy—that made it so easy for her to dive headfirst into whatever their future held.

He took her hand and tugged her down the hall. "I've

needed you in bed, naked beneath me, for forty-eight hours. I can't wait another second for you, Brooke."

No one had ever talked to her this way before, with such frank desire, drawing pictures with words that had her shuddering with pleasure as much as any caress. Seconds later, Rafe had closed her bedroom door behind them and locked it. Already she knew that the sound of a lock clicking into place would forever be a sensual cue, a promise Rafe would make to her of the pleasure he was going to give her with his hands, his lips, his—

Brooke's thoughts were stolen away as his mouth closed down over hers. God, just to kiss him like this—his tongue slicking against hers, his teeth gently nipping at her lower lip—was more pleasure than she'd ever thought to experience.

Every time until now, their kisses had been cut short, either by Rafe's conscience kicking in, or by his siblings' arrival. Tonight she would finally have enough time to truly learn not only the taste, the feel of him, but also all the ways the two of them could take their individual pleasures and multiply them together.

She flicked her tongue against the corner where his lips met, and the way his strong pectoral muscles jumped beneath her hands told her just how much he enjoyed it. Taking a slow, wet slide over his lower lip, she found the other corner and licked against it. Delight strummed through her system at the way he responded to nothing more than the damp press of her tongue. She wanted to taste more of him, so much more, but she wasn't anywhere near close to done with his lips yet.

He could easily have led their kiss, and she could feel his innate dominance even in the way he let her explore him. Sliding her hands up from his hard chest to brush over the strong lines of his neck and jaw, while the prickle of his dark five-o'clock shadow against her fingertips sent sharp bursts of pleasure down through every inch of her, she slipped her tongue between his lips on a soft moan.

Soon, the heat of their kiss took over and drew away any control either of them had been holding. Brooke couldn't get close enough, not even with her arms wrapped tightly around his neck, her breasts and stomach and hips pressed against the front of his hard body.

Rafe tore his mouth from hers. "Time to get you naked."

She wanted him naked, too, but she couldn't find the words to tell him, not when he was already teasing the patch of bare skin beneath the hem of her tank top with his fingertips, slowly pulling up the blue cotton. He'd stripped her clothes from her before, in the locked linen closet, but tonight it all felt brand-new, as if last night had only been a dress rehearsal for the real thing.

He surprised her by leaning down to press a kiss to each new inch of skin that he bared. It was glorious to be appreciated so much…but how was she possibly going to make it through to morning in one piece?

"Rafe," she whispered, and would have begged him to go faster if he hadn't responded by smiling against her stomach.

"I made a promise to you last night that the next time we did this, I'd go so slow that you'd be begging me," he murmured against her skin, his warm breath sending as many shivers through her as his words did. He lifted his dark gaze to hers. "I never break my promises."

A moment later he slid cotton up over silk so that he

could press hot kisses to the undersides of her breasts through her bra. His shoulders were strong and corded with taut tendons as she gripped him. Soon he was going to be moving up another couple of inches and his mouth would find—

Oh, God.

The whispered prayer left her lips as Rafe's lips closed over her nipple, the silk instantly wet beneath the sweet stroke of his tongue over her tightly aroused flesh. Her heartbeat raced fast and hard as he kissed his way across silk and then to the bare skin between her breasts and then over more silk to find her other nipple with his lips and tongue.

"So sweet, even through silk." He pressed a kiss to the center of her throat right before he shifted back enough to draw her tank top all the way over her head.

Brooke had lingerie that was far more revealing than this bra in light blue silk. But the way Rafe was looking at her as she stood in front of him in her simple bra and shorts made her feel as though she was wearing the sexiest undergarments ever made. And when he reached out to run the tips of two fingers across the upper curves of her breasts where her flesh rose up from the silk, she wasn't the only one shaking with need.

Badly wanting to touch him the way he was touching her, she reached for his shirt. His hands caught hers before she could lift the cotton up more than an inch.

"You're not naked yet." His eyes ran, heated, hungry, over her partially exposed breasts and waist. "Not even close."

"It's not fair," she pouted. "You already got to taste me last night." Instead of letting her yank his shirt away, he slid his fingers through hers and lifted them to his mouth to press a soft kiss against each of her knuckles. "When you do that, you make me forget."

"Forget what?" His eyes were still dark with desire, but as he teased her, they also danced with a hint of the light she'd wanted to see in him again.

Somehow she managed to remember. "That it should be my turn now."

He leaned down to cover the side of her neck with his mouth. "Tell me how you make truffles."

With the blood rushing thick and hot in her ears, she could barely make sense of his words, could only repeat, "Truffles?"

"How long does it take to get them right? To whip the chocolate into just the right consistency?"

She might have been able to follow his questions more easily were it not for the fact that he'd just found another sensitive spot on the other side of her neck.

"Can you rush the perfect sweetness, Brooke? Can you rush the perfect smoothness?" Each word fell hot and damp against a different patch of skin on her neck, the underside of her chin, and then her mouth as he licked her once, then twice as if he hadn't gotten nearly enough of a taste the first time around. "Can you rush the perfect taste of pleasure on your tongue?"

"No." She gave up her answer under sweet duress, the kind only Rafe could employ.

"You have to be patient with your truffles, don't you?"

Again, wicked persuasion was the only thing that could have drawn the *"Yes"* from her lips that was sealing her fate.

"You and I aren't going to rush anything, either," he told her as he slowly teased his fingertips down over her waist to the waistband of her shorts. "One slow, sweet orgasm at a time is how we're going to do this tonight. All night long."

Thank God he at least had enough mercy to quickly unzip her shorts and let them fall to the floor. Before they kissed, she'd already been aroused, and every kiss had ratcheted up her need higher and higher. Now Rafe's eyes caught—and held—on her matching silk panties, no longer light blue between her thighs.

"I got you all wet."

It was just what she'd said to him that first night when she'd hugged him in her wet bikini. But now, the words meant something else entirely. Something deliciously dirty that only made her wetter, especially when he put one arm around her waist to hold her steady while he reached out with the other hand to cup her through damp silk.

His eyes closed as he slowly moved his fingers over her. A muscle in his temple jumped. When his eyelids slid open again, the look he gave her was so full of desire he stole away what was left of her breath.

"How the hell am I supposed to survive this?" he asked her. "To survive you?"

"I could help make you feel better," she whispered against his neck, loving the brush of his stubble against her lips. She wanted to rub every inch of her body against him, and one day she vowed to take the lead and have him just the way he was having her now.

"So stubborn." He didn't sound at all upset about it, more pleased by what he was learning about her. "So impatient."

As if to prove him right, she rocked her pelvis into

his hand. Just a little harder, just a little longer, and she'd be—

But just as she was arching into the swell of pleasure, he took his hand away. She opened her mouth to protest, and he covered it with his lips. His mouth was hot and hard on hers as their tongues tangled again. She couldn't even come close to getting enough of him as every kiss made her desperate for another, and then another. A half dozen kisses later, she realized her bra was loose around her rib cage.

She kissed him again in a heated thank-you for stripping another piece of clothing away, and then gave a little shimmy that had the silk falling from her breasts to the floor to join her shorts and tank top.

"Better?" he asked, six little letters that liquefied her insides.

"A little, but—"

"You want more?"

"Yes." *God, yes.*

He softly cupped her breasts in his large hands. "Is this what you want?"

"Yes, and—"

Both of his thumbs stroked over her nipples, and her breath came out in a hard rush at the exquisite sensations that rippled through her.

"Good?"

Somewhere in the back of her head, she knew he was using his sexy little questions in just the same way he was using his hands, to tease her even more, to take her even closer to the edge without letting her fall all the way over.

"It's so good, but—"

"It's not enough, is it?" The corners of his mouth

curved up as she shook her head to let him know it wasn't nearly enough. "Poor baby, you must be aching so bad by now."

No one had ever had this kind of power over her, to fill her with such need that her fists were clenching against his chest as she tried to control the urge to beg. It was what he wanted, but she already knew better, knew that he'd just eat up her desperate pleas…and then likely make her wait even longer.

"Tell me," he urged, the spark dancing even brighter in his eyes now as he reveled in her sensual torture. "Are you aching, Brooke?"

She swallowed hard and tried to corral enough brain cells to hit him back with, "Are you?"

"Like never before," he confirmed, then lowered his mouth to her breasts, cupping them together so that he could lave both nipples with his tongue. "Does that help?"

"No." *God, no.*

He was so beautiful when he smiled at her that she almost forgave him for what he was doing to her, for making her *need* this much.

"What if I did this, instead?" At long last, he slid his thumbs into the sides of her panties. But instead of sliding them down, he used his leverage to pull her closer and scatter the rest of her brain cells with a kiss.

Despite her frustration at being made to wait patiently for her pleasure, how could she do anything but unclench her fists and move her hands to cup his face and kiss him back just as passionately?

As if it were her reward for good behavior, he began to inch down the final piece of silk while they kissed. When her panties were down just below her hips, and without breaking their kiss, he moved his hands from the blue silk to cup her bare bottom.

Brooke's legs automatically opened as he dragged her even closer. It was pure instinct to rub herself over the thick bulge behind the zipper of his jeans and, thank God, he didn't stop her this time. She'd never done anything this wild before, had never tried to get herself off against her lover with her panties around her thighs. Rafe's hands on her hips urged her to move higher, faster, against him and her lower belly fluttered as she came closer and closer to an explosive climax.

At the last second, Rafe stepped back. "Take your panties off and climb up on the bed."

His command was rough and as ragged as her heartbeat. She was nearly completely naked now. He was still fully clothed. She vowed to one day reverse that pattern.

But with pleasure this close, she simply slid the blue silk down to her ankles, then stepped out of her underwear to move with shaky legs over to her bed. He hadn't said how he wanted her, and she instinctively waited with a hand on the colorful quilt, looking over her shoulder in silent question.

"Jesus, Brooke. The way you're looking at me…"

He ran a hand through his hair as if she'd just pushed him too far—even though she'd done nothing more than stand naked before him. Clearly, he was doing everything he could to keep hold of what was left of his control. "I know you didn't want me to blindfold you, but maybe," she suggested in as steady a voice as she could manage, "you should blindfold *me*."

Muscles were jumping in both his jaw and temples now as he growled, "We're not going to use a damned blindfold." But she could see how much he liked the idea of it, and how hard he was trying to convince himself that he didn't. "On your back. That's how I want you. With your eyes wide open so I can see your reaction to every single thing I do to you."

A thrill shot through her at his command. Yes, it was sexy, but underlying the sheer eroticism of his words was the warmth that had always been between them, long before they'd decided to go to bed together. And, of course, he would never have asked her to do anything he didn't know for sure that she wanted, too.

She would have moved faster if she could have, but it seemed Rafe had so much power over her that even her muscles obeyed his earlier command for patience. The velvet patches sewn into the quilt felt impossibly sensuous as they brushed over her bare skin, as did the tips of her hair as they moved over her back and breasts. A heron called out for her lover from across the lake, and just as the male bird answered with a deeper call, Rafe moved onto the bed with Brooke.

His gaze roved from her face to her breasts to the slick skin between her legs. That was where they stayed and where his hands went, too, moving to her thighs so that she was completely open to him.

At last, there was no more teasing, no more need for patience as he lowered his dark head between her legs and gave her the naughtiest kiss she'd ever experienced. On a cry, she arched up into his mouth. Needing something to ground herself with when it felt like her body was shattering from the center outward, one cell at a time, Brooke clawed at the pillows, finally gripping the iron headboard for dear life.

The sound of iron creaking had Rafe looking up from between her legs. She wouldn't have believed his eyes could get any darker, could grow any fuller with desire, if she hadn't seen it right then for herself.

Because when he saw her holding on to the headboard, it was as if something snapped inside of him. And inside her, too, as the dangerous heat on his face tossed her straight to the top of the peak she'd neared so many times already...and then all the way over.

Her hips moved all on their own now, chasing ecstasy. He lowered his head again, and his tongue and lips were joined by his fingers, working together to draw her climax out. When he finally let her go limp from pleasure, she knew she was the luckiest woman on the planet as Rafe slowly kissed his way up her body.

And now it was her turn to make him feel just as good....

Fifteen

Rafe was amazed to realize that Brooke's sensuality was just as fresh and innocently seductive as the rest of her. In the same way that he'd thought he could eat just one of her chocolates last night at the bonfire. He'd nearly devoured the whole box, still hungry for more. Rafe now realized that one more perfect climax beneath his tongue wasn't anywhere close enough to filling the deep well of need he had for Brooke.

He'd *never* wanted like this.

Every moment with her was a sensual revelation. Hot. Effortless.

Perfect.

Pulling her into his arms, he kissed her mouth. "You taste good everywhere."

He felt her smile right in the center of his chest as she said, "So do you—at least, where you've let me taste."

The bright spark of fire in her eyes told him he wasn't going to be able to hold her off any longer, so when she reached for the hem of his T-shirt, he helped her get it over his head.

Her eyes were wide with clear delight as she ran

her hands slowly over his shoulders. "You're so big," she said in an awed voice that resonated straight to his groin, just like every other damned thing she'd said and done tonight. "And so hard."

Her hands were small, but he already knew how well she used them, and as her nails scraped lightly over his nipples, he sucked in a breath at the pleasure of being with her. Pleasure so big he actually forgot for a split second that—

"Rafe?" Her fingers stilled over his ribs, near a heart that was beating too hard, too fast for the beautiful woman beneath him. "What happened to you?"

Before he could respond, she was shifting so that she could see the long, jagged scar across ten inches of his skin. No one's touch had ever been as gentle.

"Who hurt you?"

"No one that matters."

But she wouldn't accept that, and when she said, again, "Who?" he knew he had to tell her the full truth, a truth almost no one else knew, including his parents.

"An ex-husband of one of my clients."

She gasped in horror, her eyes wide and furious on his behalf. "He came after you?"

Knowing it would only be worse if he waited until after they'd made love to tell her, he admitted, "After I caught him cheating on my client and when their divorce was final, I ran into her again." He wasn't proud of what he'd done, and there was a huge chance that, once she knew, Brooke might get out of the bed as quickly as she'd climbed into it. "We ended up in bed together." The flash of shock in her eyes came and went so fast, he almost thought he'd imagined it. "I was only that stupid once." He hadn't been thinking straight the night he'd broken one of his cardinal rules—*never get involved with a client*—but had simply been hoping a quick hit of physical pleasure could erase the churning in his gut over what his life had turned into. "Of course, she immediately threw it in her ex's face—that she'd slept with the man who had caught him cheating on her."

Rafe braced himself as he waited for Brooke to respond to his admission. She'd always been an open book to him before now, but suddenly he couldn't tell what she was thinking...or if she was so disgusted with him that she was a breath from ordering him from her bed.

"How dare they?" He blinked in surprise as she said, "He might have been the one to use the knife on you, but she practically handed it to him."

Rafe's breath started up again on a rush of relief... and the knowledge that he'd never done a single damn thing that was good enough to deserve Brooke's sweetness or her fierce protection of him.

"I brought it on myself."

"No, you didn't!"

He'd never heard Brooke raise her voice before, and he was suddenly reminded of the way his soft-spoken mother could emerge as a snarling tiger whenever her kids were threatened in any way. Brooke would be just as good with her own children, kids he could so easily see her playing with on the beach—jumping off the dock hand in hand with them, tucking them into bed at night with a bedtime story about princes and princesses.

He swallowed hard as he realized where his brain had gone—and how easy it had been to go there.

"You made a mistake by being with her, but they both took out their fury with each other on you." Brooke slid her arms around him, warm and strong. "And that could never be your fault."

The gash had hurt like hell that first week before dulling to a steady throb over these past couple of months. But now, for the first time since the night he'd walked into the E.R., bleeding through his shirt, he could hardly feel it. Instead, his senses were entirely captured by the steady beat of her heart against his chest, the fragrant scent of her hair, and the slick heat of her arousal against his thigh.

She pressed kisses down over his shoulder and chest, until she reached the top edge of his scar. Her lips feathered over it. "I don't ever want anyone to hurt you again," she told him as she softly kissed the length of the skin and muscle that had been stitched back together in the emergency room.

Something swelled beneath his breastbone, an emotion that was bigger than this night, bigger even than the way Brooke was healing him one kiss at a time.

She reached for the zipper of his jeans, and he let her pull the denim down, but when his erection jumped beneath the light stroke of her fingers over cotton, he knew better than to let her pull off his boxers, too. All it would take was the slightest touch of her fingertips over him, and he'd lose it.

A few seconds after removing his boxers himself, he kicked off his last piece of clothing and both of them were finally naked. He kissed her and reveled in the amazing feeling of her bare skin sliding against his for the first time.

His.

She was *his.*

The thought was echoing over and over in his head when she told him, "I'm ready now."

Slowly caressing her gorgeous curves, moving his hand over her breasts, waist, hips and inner thighs, he finally slicked his fingers through her wetness. She arched into his touch, and he bit down on her earlobe.

"Baby, you're more than ready."

He stroked her again, moving his fingers inside of her in just the right way to make her grip his shoulders more tightly as her inner muscles clenched hard over him. Her mouth was sweet against his as he kissed her with the ferocity that hc wouldn't usc in the thrust of his hand up against her.

"Soon," he promised her, knowing what she really wanted…his body moving into her, hard against soft. "But only after you come again for me at least one more time."

He matched the rhythm of his tongue against hers with the plunge of his fingers into her incredibly welcoming body. He'd always loved women and sex, but nothing he'd ever experienced before compared to being with Brooke. No woman he'd ever been with had been so pure in her sensuality, so willing to give herself over to his touch, to the press of his lips on her, to the stroke of his fingertips across every sensitive patch of skin, both inside and out.

She was still trembling, still pulsing over his hand as she said, "That feels so good, Rafe." She cupped his face in her hands and pulled his mouth back down to hers, kissing him in her sweetly seductive way.

He could have watched, listened to, felt her come all night long. But both of them had been more than patient for the past two days. Shifting away from her just enough to reach the condoms he'd pulled out of his jeans, he was about to rip one of the packages open when Brooke said, "Now that I did what you told me to," she said with that sexy spark in her eyes, "I can't wait to be kinky with you."

Forgetting all about the condom in his hand, Rafe almost exploded right then and there. God, she had no idea how close he was to taking her hips in his hands and thrusting into her to lose himself in her softness, in her beauty, in the look in her eyes that told him he could do absolutely anything he wanted with her.

No. Damn it, he needed to stay in control. Somehow, some way, he needed to remember that Brooke was different. Special.

And far more precious than any woman he'd ever been with.

"I told you," he somehow managed to grit out, "I'm not going to do that kind of stuff to you."

Her full lower lip pouted slightly at him, and he had to nip at it, even as she said, "But I want you to." Sweet Lord, she needed to stop saying those things, but then she added, "You told me last night you'd make me beg."

"No, Brooke," he pleaded with her, "don't beg me."

Everything stilled between them in that moment as she looked up at him, her eyes full of desire, but also clear...and decided.

"Be wild with me." She stroked her hands down his chest, her nails lightly scoring his chest. *"Please."*

Rafe had never been particularly gentle in bed, but he wanted to be gentle with Brooke. Tender, too, because of how special she was to him.

Of course, the irony was that just when he was trying to be gentle and tender, she was asking for wild. For kinky.

Still intent on doing whatever he needed to do to resist her pleas, though he wanted that wildness just as badly as she did, when she reached for his shaft, the only way he could keep the game from being over right then and there was to grab her wrists and pull them as far away from his erection as he could.

It was in that exact moment that he gripped her arms tightly above her head—a throaty moan leaving her lips as if he were already inside of her   that Rafe realized the power Brooke had over him.

He'd vowed not to let himself go crazy, had sworn that he wouldn't let himself forget to be gentle. He could never forgive himself for stealing Brooke's wide-eyed innocence, for sullying any part of her sweetness.

But the way she was begging was more than enough to drive a guy crazy…and to have him losing what was left of his patience.

Needing her *now,* Rafe used his knees and thighs to push her legs open wide, and then wider still. She writhed sensuously beneath him, her eyes cloudy with desire, her pretty mouth plump from the kisses with which he'd ravaged them, her skin flushed with arousal, her breasts so full and soft and sweet that he had to close his mouth over one peak again.

He pulled back from her breast with a scrape of his teeth over her sensitive flesh that had her begging again. Her words shouldn't have made any sense—*Need. Please. Take. Want*—but he had no trouble deciphering them at all because they were the same ones playing on repeat in his head.

He'd planned on taking her slowly. He'd warned himself to be gentle with her. But as her heat, her scent, the sweet taste of her mouth pushed him to the edge, with her wrists still tightly restrained above her head in one of his hands, Rafe used the other to shove on the condom. He pushed into her in one hard stroke, so deep that she gasped aloud.

Oh, God, I've hurt her.

He tried to still himself inside of her, but before he could manage anything even close to it, or apologize for being too rough, she was moving beneath him, her soft curves and muscles working hard to take him even deeper. Her neck was arched back, her eyelids fluttering, her strong fingers opening, then clenching above where he was holding her wrists. A sheen of sweat gleamed on her skin, and he could have sworn she was glowing.

Just as her inner muscles began to pulse around him, her lips curved up into a smile. One so full of bliss, so pure and heartfelt, he could hardly believe he was lucky enough to be the one to see it…and to be the man who had made her that happy.

Watching her giving herself up entirely to pleasure and perfect joy beneath him, Rafe couldn't do anything but give himself up to the unbelievable pleasure, too.

No longer holding anything back, he thrust into her hard, and then harder still. Sweat dripped from his body to hers, one drop running down between her breasts as wet skin rubbed against wet skin.

"Now, Brooke." Her eyes flew open, so dilated with arousal that the black of her pupils had pushed out nearly all of the green. *"Now."*

As if she'd simply been waiting for his command,

before either of them could take their next breath, she was exploding beneath him, around him, holding nothing back at all as her climax rocked them both.

Sixteen

"That *was* better than chocolate!"

Rafe lifted his head from the crook of her neck. "How much better?"

Uh-oh, she hadn't realized she'd said the words aloud. But how could she be embarrassed with him after how close they'd been? How close they still were, actually, with his wonderfully large body pressing hers into the mattress.

"*Way* better," she replied. "Especially that last part."

He looked surprised when he saw that he was still holding her arms over her head, almost as if he hadn't realized he'd done it at all. Cool air rushed over her wrists as he quickly let her go. "Did I hurt you?"

She frowned at his question. "Of course you didn't." But when she looked at her wrists, she could clearly see the imprints of his fingers across her skin.

"Damn it, I did."

She shook her head. "No, it's just that I'm so pale. My skin always marks a little when something's pressed up against it, but it disappears really fast."

When he got up to throw away the condom, she knew

he was going to blame himself for something he hadn't done, but she wouldn't let him do it.

She reached out for him. "Come back to bed, Rafe."

Standing in the moonlight shining through her bedroom window, she watched him fight with himself for a few seconds, that muscle jumping in his jaw again. Finally, he moved back toward her and took her hand.

She drew him back onto the bed and made him lie on his back so that she could settle into the crook of his shoulder. "I love every single thing we did together. When you were holding on to my wrists like that," she whispered, "I felt freer than I ever have before." She lifted her gaze to meet his as she added, "And I can't wait to do even more next time."

She watched a new flash of heat jump in his eyes before he tamped it down. "Having your wrists in my hands is as kinky as we're going to get, Brooke."

She could have argued with him, could have told him he wasn't going to win this one. Instead, she simply smiled and said, "You finally said 'kinky.'"

In the darkened room, the smile was still on her lips as she ran her fingertips lightly over his scar, then laid her palm flat over his beating heart and closed her eyes.

Rafe couldn't believe he'd fallen asleep in Brooke's bed. Morning light streamed in over him, and he worked to get his sluggish mind to click into gear. When Brooke had wrapped her arms around him and snuggled close, his entire body had desperately craved her softness, her warmth…and the sense that she was healing the broken parts of him one kiss at a time.

Still, he was amazed that not only had sex with Brooke been super crazy hot, but she was just the same afterward as she'd been before. Full of smiles and the sweetness that had always been such a big part of her, and *no* talk about feelings.

He could hear the shower running, and knew he should leave her to finish washing up alone, especially after the way he'd taken her last night—hard enough that she might be sore. But Rafe was quickly learning that he didn't have any control where Brooke was concerned. Especially when the thought of her naked and wet and soapy in the shower had him as hard as he'd ever been, as if he hadn't just lost himself inside her less than eight hours ago.

The bathroom door was unlocked, but he wouldn't have thought twice about picking the lock to get to her. The room was steamy, the glass door of the shower fogged up, so that all he could see was a gorgeous outline of skin and curves and long, wet hair.

"Rafe?"

He answered by opening the shower door and stepping under the water with her, dropping the protection he'd brought with him on the tiled bench.

Her happy smile was immediate, as were her hands coming around his shoulders when she drew him close to her for a kiss to start the morning. Every time they kissed, he was shocked to realize he wanted her more.

Last night should have begun to take the edge off. Instead, the opposite was true.

"I didn't want to wake you when you were sleeping so soundly," she said against his lips, "but I'm really glad you're up now."

"You can wake me anytime for this."

Thirty seconds was as long as it would have taken for him to have her pressed up against the tiles, her legs wrapped around his waist. But that would have meant missing out on the chance to run the bar of soap over every inch of her skin.

Her eyes went wide and her breath came faster as he moved around her body so that he was standing behind her. The water had plastered her long hair to her neck and back, and Rafe thoroughly enjoyed lifting the soaked strands up and over one shoulder. Beneath the spray of the shower, the ends of her dirty-blond hair had darkened to the color of her flushed nipples.

Aroused by the sweet curve of her neck, he dropped his mouth to her delicate skin. She shivered as he pressed his lips against her, and then his tongue.

Her hands reached out as if she needed to hold on to something and pressed up flat against the cool lake-blue tiles. "Stay just like that," he encouraged her, loving the way she sucked in a shaky breath at his words.

Slowly, he began to run the bar of soap across her shoulders, her upper back, then down to the perfect indentation of her waist, just above the sweet flare of her gorgeous hips. Her body was a miracle, soft where a woman should be soft, full where a woman should be full and strong in a way he hadn't known many women to be strong.

Not to mention her innate sensuality, powerful enough to nearly break a man who had never let himself come anywhere close to being broken by a woman before.

Her skin was smooth and perfect beneath his fingertips, and he was mesmerized by the way the bubbles slid across her curves. Temporarily putting down the soap, he cupped his hands to gather water and pour it over her.

When her soft moan reverberated off the tiled walls

and floor, he did it again, only this time he spilled the water over the front of her shoulders so that it ran in hot rivulets between her breasts. She began to move away from the wall with the clear intention of wrapping herself around him, but he laid his hands flat over hers on the tiles to still her.

"Not yet, sweetheart. I'm not even close to getting you clean."

Enjoying her soft sound of frustration just as much as he had her moan of pleasure, he picked up the soap again and moved to press his erection against her hips, his chest to her back. Of course, she knew exactly how to get her revenge on him for making her be patient. She wiggled her sweet, round ass into him, making him throb so hard against her that he nearly lost it.

"Are you sure you want to play with me like that?" His low words held a clear, yet sensual, warning that she should be careful how far she pushed a man like him.

"God, yes."

It was what she'd said to him last night when he was teasing her, and as she wiggled herself against him again Rafe lowered his cheek to the top of her wet hair and breathed in her fresh, clean scent, letting it fill him up.

A moment later he was sliding both hands around to make soapy circles around her belly button. How could he keep teasing her like this when it was just as much torture for him not to touch the rest of her?

Giving himself over to pleasure was so much easier. And better, too, as he began to soap up the heavy undersides of her breasts.

"Please," she begged, even though he'd already

dropped the soap so that he could pinch her erect nipples between each thumb and forefinger.

"Shh," he soothed against her earlobe before he nipped at it.

A hard shudder worked through her as he slid one hand back down to her belly, and then down lower still, until the damp curls between her legs were tickling his fingertips. They moved together in perfect sync, her legs opening wider just as his hand found her flesh slick and so damned hot that he didn't have a prayer of holding back one more second.

He quickly spun her around and pressed her against the tiles with the weight of his body as he ripped open the condom, only stepping back enough from her luscious curves to shove the latex down over himself. And then he was lifting her up so that she was wrapping her arms and legs around him, and he was thrusting into her in one hard stroke that stole the breath from both their lungs.

She was small but strong as she pulled him closer. Every time they were together, he vowed to be more careful with her the next time. But need had him spiraling out of control again, and apart from protecting her soft curves and the back of her head with his hands against the hard tile, he couldn't do a damned thing to stop himself from pounding into her, or from kissing her hard enough to bruise her lips.

Yet again, she surprised him not only by taking everything he gave her, but also by encouraging him to go further. Because instead of crying out at the rough way he was taking her with absolutely no finesse or gentleness at all, her soft laughter ricocheted through the shower. Even as her inner muscles tightened down around him and she used her strong thigh and arm muscles to work herself over him, the beautifully wild woman in his arms was not only smiling...she was actually laughing out loud with clear joy.

Every time she laughed, Rafe felt it in the center of his chest. But never more than now, when what should have been fast, furious lovemaking had turned into something else entirely. Something that eased the tightening in his chest even more than loving her had last night.

Before Brooke, sex had only been about momentary pleasure.

With Brooke, he finally realized how much joy there could be in it, too.

"I love the sound of your laughter," he told her, and he was smiling, too, as he covered her mouth with his. He was amazed that even as laughter turned back to moans and gasps, the joy that she'd wrapped all around him never let go, not for one second.

When her body exploded in climax, Rafe didn't have a prayer of holding back his own release. And why would he, when nothing had ever felt better than jumping off the edge with her?

They clung to each other for several minutes afterward as they both worked to catch their breath, and when he finally put her back down on her feet, she was grinning up at him.

"That was *awesome!*" She sounded just the way she had when they'd ridden his motorcycle into town, utterly exhilarated and thrilled by her discovery of what a rush speed could be.

Rafe agreed wholeheartedly—making love to her in the shower had easily been the most awesome moment of his life—but at the same time, he couldn't push away another chorus of self-condemnation over the way he kept losing control with her.

"What are you doing to me?"

She reached for his jaw with one hand and stroked it. His wet stubble rasped under her fingertips. "Well, right now, I'm going to shave you." She went on her tippy-toes to move her mouth closer to his. "We can figure out the rest later."

He didn't know how she did it—how she took something that could have been so complicated and made it simple. Easy.

Right.

She had him sit on the tiled seat at the back of the shower and filled her palm with shaving cream. All it took was the soft brush of her fingers over his neck and jaw for him to grow hard again. Damn it, he couldn't let himself take her again.

Misinterpreting his grimace as concern, she said, "I promise I'll be gentle," and then she was picking up the razor and moving her legs on either side of his so that her gorgeous chest was right at tongue level. Did she know how much she was torturing him as she tilted his head back so that she could run the razor over his neck?

He'd done a lot of wild things in his life, but he'd never thought one of the wildest would be having the most beautiful girl in the world straddling him in the shower while she shaved him, her lower lip between her teeth in deep concentration.

The only thing that stopped him from grabbing her and tugging her all the way onto his lap—and the erection that wouldn't quit whenever she was near—was knowing how bad she'd feel if her hand slipped and she cut him. He was more than willing to shed a little blood to have her again, but he forced himself to keep his hands resting lightly on the outsides of her thighs as she deftly moved the razor up to his jaw.

When she was done, she quickly rinsed him clean with water from the shower spout. She leaned down and rubbed her cheek against his. "Mmm, so smooth."

No longer needing to worry about the razor, he stood up, shut off the water and took her with him from the bathroom into the bedroom, both of them dripping as they hit the bed and fell on it together. He'd never trusted any woman to do something as intimate as shave him, but with Brooke it had felt like the way things were supposed to be. Just as it did when he rolled them over so that she was straddling him on the bed and he could nuzzle her breasts with his freshly shaven face.

"Mmm," he murmured against her sweet-smelling skin, "so smooth."

She was laughing at the way he'd used her own words on her as he grabbed another condom from beside the bed, then pulled her down over him. He could feel her joy in the throb of her inner muscles against him with each burst of laughter from her lungs. He wasn't a teenager anymore, and after having her twice in less than twelve hours, he should have been able to last a little longer.

But the way Brooke looked riding him—beyond gorgeous with her head thrown back, wet hair streaming down her back, lost to ecstasy with her hands gripping his forearms—crushed any control he should have had. He could feel every catch of her breath, every gasp of pleasure when he thrust into her and hit just the right spot.

He wanted to watch her come, but he needed to taste

her some more. Sitting up, he slid his hands into her wet hair and kissed her. He'd never experienced need this fierce, this consuming. All that existed was Brooke, the smooth slick of her tongue against his, the grip of her hands across his shoulders as her climax hit her hard enough that all she could do was press her cheek against his and hold on tight.

Rafe forced himself to unwrap his arms from around Brooke so that she could get dressed. But instead of putting on jeans, she took a pretty dress from her closet, along with even prettier lingerie to wear beneath it.

At his unspoken question, she told him, "I spoke with Cord before I got in the shower. He needs me to come into the city today to do a walk-through on the new storefront and sign some papers."

Rafe's gut tightened at nothing more than the sound of another man's name on her lips. He didn't much care for the idea of her being away from him for so many hours, either. All these years he'd been wary of women who clung too tight, who wanted to be together every free second, yet here he was feeling exactly that way with Brooke.

"I'm sure Mia would love to have you stay with her while you're in town. Or," he told her instead of begging her to stay the way he wanted to, "you could use my place."

She smiled at the offer, but shook her head. "I'm not planning to stay in Seattle tonight."

Though he was silently rejoicing at the thought of having Brooke back in his arms by nightfall, he said, "I don't want you to be so tired after your meetings that you have trouble driving back to the lake."

Her chin lifted, but she gave him one of her sweet smiles. "I'll be fine, Rafe." Her gaze heated up as she added, "And I don't want to spend the night in the city, not when I'd much rather be here in bed with you tonight."

"How about I come with you?" He'd like to meet this Cord guy, and see what his gut told him about the man who'd managed to sign himself up as Brooke's business partner so easily.

"No," she said with a shake of her head, "you're just hitting your stride on fixing up your house. And this is your vacation."

She was right, but she meant a hell of a lot more to him than some house ever would. He was about to insist when she cut him off at the pass with, "Honestly, I'll be totally fine on my own."

Knowing it was her gentle way of telling him to back off, and trying to respect her wishes despite his concerns for her, he made sure she had his cell phone number just in case she needed anything at all, then pulled on his jeans and went out to the kitchen to make her breakfast before she hit the road. Lord knew they'd expended more than enough energy since last night. But instead of sitting down with him she simply told him she was already late, thanked him for the bagel he'd toasted and buttered for her, threw several boxes of her chocolates into a big canvas bag, then kissed him once before flying out the door looking stunning in her wrap dress and heels.

Rafe stood in the middle of her kitchen feeling as if he'd just been hit by a hurricane.

He'd had plenty of good sex in the past fifteen years, but nothing anywhere close to as hot as what he and

Brooke had shared. Sure, he was just a clueless guy, as his sister had pointed out at least a hundred times to him over the years, but he hadn't missed the fact that even in the midst of the heat between him and Brooke, there'd been something more.

And, instead of angling for a commitment or wanting to define whether they'd shifted into officially being boyfriend/girlfriend now, she'd hopped into her car and headed to the city alone.

Hell, he thought, as he ran his hands roughly through his hair, he'd practically begged to tag along. But she very clearly hadn't wanted him to come with her.

He chewed the situation over. Was it because she didn't want him to meet her business partner? He hated to admit it, but he had developed an irrational hatred for the guy just by hearing his name. What kind of legitimate businessman was named Cord? After pulling out his phone and doing a search on the guy, Rafe didn't much care for the way he looked, either. Why the hell did her partner have to be so good-looking?

He thought about Brooke hooking up with the man, but he couldn't get a clear vision of it for one really good reason: She would never, in a million years, leave his bed to go to anyone else's. Rafe was a cynical bastard, but he wasn't blind. Brooke had surprised him over and over during the past few days, but she wasn't, and would never be, a cheater.

While he wasn't worried about her hooking up with her business partner behind his back, he was still worried. Particularly with regard to the money she was continuing to hand over. She was too smart to walk naïvely into a business partnership with a stranger, and while he assumed she'd done her due diligence on the guy, the truth was that Rafe and his employees could find out things about Cord that she never could. Particularly if her new partner had anything he was trying to hide.

It was one thing for Brooke to risk her hard-earned money on her own talent—which she had in spades. It was another entirely for her to risk it on someone else.

Angry with himself for not making this phone call earlier—he'd been so wrapped up in wanting Brooke, and then when he'd failed to keep a handle on that need he'd been even more caught up in taking her every which way he could—Rafe's voice was gruff as Ben picked up at the office.

"Hey, boss, I hope you're calling me from a fishing boat to brag about your latest catch."

Normally he would have shot the shit with his employee, who was also a longtime friend. But today Brooke was all that mattered. "I need you to check into a guy named Cord Delacorte."

Ben immediately switched into business mode. "Anything you're looking for in particular?"

"I want to know everything about the guy."

Ben knew precisely what *everything* meant in their business: where Cord went and who he went with, everything he bought, everyone he called, and where his money was coming from and going to as far back as they could trace his activities.

"I'll make this my top priority and will both call and email you immediately with anything that looks suspicious."

With Brooke in Seattle, Rafe had nothing to distract him from putting in the rest of his new flooring, along with the kitchen cabinets that were being delivered today. But instead of being glad to have so many uninterrupted hours to set his lake house to rights, he was already counting down the minutes and hours.

Not for sex this time, but simply for the chance to see Brooke's smiling face…and to hold her in his arms.

Seventeen

Brooke stood on the muggy main street in Kirkland at dusk and waved goodbye to Cord and his wife. Just as Rafe had predicted, Brooke was exhausted. The hours she'd already put in driving to Seattle, combined with actually signing the papers for the storefront with the lawyer and Realtor, would have been tiring enough. But doing all of that after making love with Rafe for half the night and then twice this morning had left her with rubbery limbs and a mind that kept drifting back to him. On top of that, after a quick wrap-up drink with Cord and his wife in which she'd learned more about their fertility problems, she dearly wished she could help them in some way. They were clearly deeply in love with each other and desperately wanted a child, but all the love and wanting in the world hadn't yet made a difference.

Love. She'd always thought it could make magic happen. But could it?

Yet again, her thoughts swung around to Rafe, just as they had every other minute or two during her long day. From the first moment she'd seen him get off his motorcycle and look at her with his darkly intense eyes, she'd wanted him. Needed him, woman to man. From the way he'd touched her, kissed her, made love to her, she knew he wanted and needed her in just the same way. But it was everything he'd told her about his job, and the scar he wore across his ribs, that made her believe he needed her for something more than just the quenching of desire. For more, even, than friendship.

For love?

A young boy whizzing by on a skateboard had her jumping out of the way with a hand over her racing heart. Of course, it had already been racing from the mere thought of falling in love with Rafe....

Reminding herself that nothing was certain about their relationship going forward, that they purposely hadn't made any promises to each other beyond making sure they didn't hurt their friendship, Brooke refocused her attention on the present. She had one more very important errand at an address she'd looked up on her phone earlier that day. In fact, she was hoping to bring a present home to Rafe tonight.

Brooke was impressed with the front window of Indulgence. While she and Mia had been painting Rafe's living room, Mia had told her all about the incredible new store just down the street from where Brooke's new store would be. Indulgence was owned by one of Mia's closest girlfriends, a woman named Colbie, who believed every woman should not only indulge herself, but the man in her life, as well. And when Mia had mentioned that the store carried a few things in her Members Only room that were so naughty even *she* hadn't bought them for herself, Brooke had made a mental note to pay a visit to the store on her next trip to Seattle.

Downtown Kirkland, with its abundance of children's toy shops and housewares stores and cafes, wasn't the kind of place a girl went to find supersexy lingerie, or so Brooke had always thought. She walked in, and a beautiful woman immediately greeted her with a warm smile.

"Hello, how are you doing tonight?"

Brooke immediately felt at ease with the woman behind the register. "I'm doing great, thanks. Are you Colbie?"

"I am. And you're one of Mia's friends, aren't you?" When Brooke nodded, Colbie laughed. "I don't even know why I pay for advertising when she's better at spreading the word than any newspaper or magazine could ever be."

"Mia raved about your store." She looked around at the beautiful merchandise on tasteful display. "I can see that she was right. I'm Brooke."

Colbie's grin grew even wider. "You're her childhood friend from the lake—the one the Sullivans used to visit! I can't tell you how thrilled she is to have found you again after all these years."

"I'm thrilled, too." Brooke suddenly realized that by coming here and saying who she was, Colbie might very well know precisely which man she was shopping for.

"Can I help you find something specific, or would you like me to leave you alone so you can browse in peace?"

"Actually—" Brooke felt her face flush and she covered her cheeks with her hands to try to hide it.

"Do you want to see what I've got in my Members Only room?" Colbie guessed.

"I do."

The other woman grinned at her. "I knew I liked you, right from the moment you walked inside. Follow me."

As they headed past a gauzy curtain, Brooke felt her face heating up again, but she was here, wasn't she? She needed to be brave enough to follow through with her purchase.

She'd seen pictures of some of the merchandise in the velvet-lined display cases, but even though the very sexy products Colbie carried were actually quite elegant, Brooke just couldn't see herself wearing or using any of them. She wanted Rafe to understand that her boundaries were further out than he obviously thought they were, but she also needed to stay true to herself.

Besides, he hadn't needed anything but his hands over her wrists last night....

"Let me know if you have any questions," Colbie offered.

Brooke's eyes had caught on one possibility. "Tell me more about these."

Colbie grinned as she ran the length of colorful silk between her fingertips. "My fiancé loves these. So many possibilities…" She was interrupted right then by the sound of a man's low voice from the other side of the curtain, and she literally glowed with happiness at hearing it. "Noah is a little early to pick me up for dinner, but I'll tell him to relax for a while."

But Brooke had already made up her mind. "I'll take the silks." She pointed at the lingerie on the mannequin. "That, too, if you've got it in my size."

Brooke went out into the main room and met Colbie's sinfully gorgeous fiancé, Noah Bryant. The way he looked at Colbie, as though she were brighter than the sun, the moon and the stars combined, had Brooke barely containing her sigh at how sweet they were.

Was there any chance that Rafe would ever look at her that way?

Or maybe, just maybe, if Mia was to be believed, was there a chance that he already did?

Rafe had just finished laying the final floorboard when his phone rang. He hoped it was Brooke letting him know she was on her way home.

But it wasn't. Instead, his cousin Sophie's name lit up the screen.

Always glad to hear from one of his many cousins, he picked up. "Hey, Soph, how are you, Jake and the kids doing?" He could hear a baby girl's laughter in the background, and then her husband Jake's booming laugh a moment later.

"Amazing," she answered. "And loud. Really, really loud, if you hadn't noticed."

Sophie's nickname was *Nice*. On top of that, she was a librarian, so she was used to working in a quiet space all day. He imagined marriage to the owner of a chain of Irish pubs, and then having twins, had taken some getting used to. Clearly, though, she was happy with the huge changes to her life, especially since Sophie and Jake had been in love with each other since they were kids.

It wasn't, he suddenly realized, too different from his situation with Brooke. Sophie and Jake had known each other since she was five or six; Rafe had known Brooke even longer than that. And then one day Sophie and Jake had gone from being family friends to much, much more, just as Rafe and Brooke had. The only difference was that where Jake McCann had changed from not wanting a serious relationship to happily marrying and having a family with Sophie, Rafe and Brooke were simply having a good time with each other.

It was only a summer fling, just for fun, wasn't it?

Belatedly, he realized Sophie was talking.

"—call with Mia the other day, and she told me you bought back your family's lake house. I'm so happy for you, and actually that's partly why I'm calling. We're planning on taking a vacation later this summer, and once your sister told me about the lake it sounded like the perfect retreat from our everyday nuttiness. Plus, I could see you and stop by Seattle to see the rest of your family, too. Do you know if there are any cottages or vacation rentals available?"

"Stay here, at my place."

"Are you sure? The four of us can be a lot to live with, even for just a few days."

"You can have the place to yourself."

"We couldn't kick you out of your own summer house."

"It's okay," he reassured her, "I'm sure I can stay next door."

"So," his cousin said, drawing out the two letters, "then it sounds like Mia's right. You and Brooke are officially—"

"Nothing's official," he quickly clarified, "but Brooke's a good friend, and I'm sure she'll have no problem with me crashing at her place, especially if she gets to see you and your family."

But even as he said it, the words didn't sound quite right in his head, didn't feel quite right falling off his tongue. Because he wasn't "crashing" with Brooke anymore, and even though it was true that nothing was official, that didn't make what they'd shared so far feel any less powerful, any less potent.

He heard a shriek in the background and then the phone dropped as Sophie said, "Oh, Smith, honey, it's okay." When she picked the phone up, he could hear her little boy crying. "Sorry about that, Rafe. Like I said, never a dull moment. Oh, and before I go, Jake wants you to know he's got some awesome new beer he's been brewing that he'll bring for you."

"Give everyone a hug and a kiss for me, Soph. And as soon as you figure out the dates for your vacation, consider my place yours."

Rafe wouldn't have thought he could envy a guy who'd once had his pick of any woman he wanted, and who was now having to deal with a wife and two babies. But, right then, it seemed to Rafe that Jake McCann was the luckiest bastard in the world.

Just under three hours later, Brooke stumbled in her front door. She'd heard the drill going at Rafe's house when she'd gotten out of her car, and even though she was dying to see him, she was also desperate for another shower to wash away the slight aches from her long drive.

It always felt so good to come back to the lake, even after only a day away. But today she was thankful for far more than the beautiful lake with the waning moon beginning to rise over it.

She'd had a lot of time to think in the car. It was, in fact, the main reason she'd wanted to make the trip alone. Of course she would have loved to have spent the time with Rafe, but her head had been spinning so fast after they'd made love yet again on the bed that morning, still wet from the shower.

Too fast?

How, she wondered, could everything change so quickly?

Or, she'd asked herself over and over again as the miles rolled beneath the tires, had anything really changed at all?

Yes, they were no longer platonic friends, having transitioned pretty darned completely into friends-with-benefits. But beyond that, had there been something more than just heat in his eyes when he'd gazed down at her as he was making love to her?

Were the emotions she'd thought she could hear in his voice when he whispered her name really there? Or was she simply imagining what she so desperately wanted to see and hear…and feel…from him?

For tonight, she'd decided it would have to be enough to push at his sensual boundaries. She'd focus on fighting one battle at a time.

And the first thing would be to give every last ounce of pleasure they could to each other.

And then, if she was even luckier, she'd win his heart.

Unlike the long, hot shower she and Rafe had taken together that morning, now she quickly shampooed and soaped up before rinsing off and getting out to towel off. Normally, slipping back into her jeans and a T-shirt after wearing a tailored dress and heels all day in the city felt like coming home. But she wasn't planning on putting her jeans back on tonight.

Before she left Colbie's store, she'd bought not only the gorgeous lengths of silk, but also the prettiest—and sexiest—lingerie she'd ever seen. She'd bought it with thoughts of how Rafe would react when he saw her in it, but as she pulled the exquisite lace and silk out of the shopping bag, she realized it would thrill *her* just as much to wear it. She'd never given too much thought to her undergarments before, but after spending a little time in Indulgence she had to wonder if this could be yet another way of giving rein to her wild side, with sensual secrets that only she and her lover would know were waiting beneath her clothes.

She was wearing her secret beneath a simple blue cotton summer dress and had laid her other purchase out over the pillows when she heard Rafe walk in the front door ten minutes later. But as she walked out into the living room, and he met her halfway to tug her into his arms, she immediately forgot about secrets and her day in Seattle.

All she could think about was how good it felt to be back in his arms.

Eighteen

God, he'd missed her today.

When Rafe heard Brooke drive up, he'd wanted to drop his tools, pull her out of the driver's seat and kiss her senseless, but he'd forced himself to give her a few minutes to decompress first.

Four days ago she hadn't been in his life.

Four days ago he could have made it through a twelve-hour stretch without longing for her.

Four days ago he hadn't had the slightest clue just how much his life was going to be completely rocked by a beautiful girl with innocent eyes and soft curves.

But here she was, standing before him.

Her hair was still just the slightest bit damp from the shower. He could have stood with her and breathed in her sweet, fresh scent for hours.

"How were your meetings?"

"Good." She lifted her face from his chest. "I missed you today."

His heart squeezed. The women he'd been with before Brooke had either played hard to get, or had pressured him for more than he'd had any intention of giving. But he knew she was simply telling him what she felt, with no ulterior motives.

He lowered his mouth to hers and told her with his kiss just how much he'd missed her, too. And yet, though all he could think about was taking her to bed for a repeat of their earlier lovemaking, he made himself pull back. "You must be exhausted from your trip."

"I was," she admitted, "but now that you're here, I'm not anymore."

Sweet Lord, all he wanted was to drag her into the bedroom, tear her clothes off, and take her fast and hard. Instead, he asked, "Are you hungry?"

Her lips curved up into a small smile. "Yes."

Damn it, somehow he was going to have to make it through a meal without losing what was left of his mind.

But then she was pressing her body against his and saying, "Hungry for you."

How could he do anything but love her mouth the way he wanted to love the rest of her? When he finally let her up for air, and both of them were panting, she licked her lips, already damp from his tongue.

"There's something I want to show you."

Rafe warned himself it could be anything. Pictures of her new storefront. A new style of box she'd found to package chocolates. Even, possibly, the contracts she'd signed today. But the way she'd said the words *There's something I want to show you* had Rafe only able to think about sexy things.

Dirty things.

When she slid her hands into his and took him back into the bedroom, he immediately noticed several strips of colored silk draped across the pillows. To the naked eye they looked like scarves. But Rafe knew exactly what they were for.

They were sensual bindings meant for a woman's naked skin, and he went a little crazy just thinking about using them with Brooke.

"Where did you get those?"

As she picked up the silks, sweetness shimmered in her eyes alongside a budding wickedness that kept surprising him, over and over.

"In a really fun store in Seattle."

The vision of Brooke browsing through sex toys had Rafe nearly bursting the zipper of his jeans. But this was just the kind of thing he'd sworn he wouldn't do to her. She'd been a good girl before him, and he doubted she would ever have walked into the store before they'd started sleeping together.

Forcing himself to shove aside the too-clear vision of using the scarves to bind her to the iron head- and footboards, her beautiful body naked and open to him, he said, "I already told you we don't need props."

Though his voice was rough, when he pulled her back into his arms a moment later, making the silk fall from her fingers as her hands slid over his shoulders, his lips were gentle over hers. She sighed into his mouth, making one of her little sounds of pleasure that had been playing on repeat inside his head all day long.

He gathered the fabric of her dress in his hands and pulled it up. But when he got to her hips, he had to smooth his hands over her hips and thighs. Lace and silk and soft, smooth skin met his palms and fingertips. She pleased him, every part of her, so much that he couldn't wait any longer to strip her dress all the way off. Only, once her dress was on the floor, Rafe had to try like hell to pick his jaw up off it, too.

Strips of see-through white lace and silk crisscrossed her body, leaving her at once covered and naked...and so damned beautiful that he was stunned senseless.

"I also bought this today," she told him in a husky voice. "Do you like it?"

But he couldn't speak just yet, couldn't do anything but reach for her again to run his fingertips down over the fabric that started at her shoulders, then curved over her incredible breasts. Her nipples beaded beneath his hands, and she pressed herself into his palms. Yet again, she was pure sensuality come to life as he followed the strips down across her stomach to where they met over her gorgeous bottom.

Again and again he'd vowed to curb his natural impulses with her, but now he wondered how the hell he'd ever have a prayer of doing that.

Any self-control he had left was on its last legs as his fingers slowly continued their trip over silk and lace. And when he finally cupped his hand between her legs, he learned that the shockingly sexy lingerie didn't cover everything after all.

Damp, hot skin met his fingers instead of lace and silk. Whispering his name against his mouth, Brooke rolled her hips so that his fingers stroked over, then into the heart of her. Just that fast, she was coming for him, and the joy he felt when her climax tore through her was unlike anything he'd ever felt before.

Brooke.

Only with Brooke.

Oh, my.

Brooke's new sexy lingerie had inspired quite a response from Rafe…one that had her tingling from head to toe. But there were other things she wanted, too. Things that involved not only the naughty lingerie she was wearing, but also the silk bindings she'd bought in Seattle. Things that Rafe, quite obviously, had no intention of giving her.

Maybe it was better that way. Since he had such a big thing about not wanting to "strip away her innocence," she'd take any room for potential guilt out of his hands by stripping it away herself.

Perhaps it was knowing just how powerfully he'd been moved by her sexy lingerie that made it feel perfectly natural to drop to her knees in front of him. She couldn't help but smile at the way he was frowning down at her.

"Brooke—"

"Shh," she said to him, just as he'd done with her when they were in the shower and she'd been begging him not to tease her. She didn't need to feel him beneath the zipper of his jeans to know how hard he was, but when she undid his fly and slowly slid his jeans down, though she'd already been with him more than once, she was surprised all over again at just how big he was. Her mouth already watering, she didn't just pull down the denim, but made sure to bring his boxers down, too.

"Oh, Rafe." She didn't try to hide her delight at just how beautiful he was.

One of her hands rose automatically to wrap around him, and he throbbed hard once, then twice against her palm and fingers. "Come to the bed with me, Brooke."

But she didn't want to do that—not unless he was willing to play with her the way she guessed he'd played with his other lovers. In some ways, she knew she had more of him than any of his previous lovers had—their friendship, their past, their family connections. But in other ways, she knew she had less.

She wouldn't settle for that, darn it, whatever good reasons he thought he had for the way he was behaving, for believing she couldn't handle his darker desires...or her own. She wouldn't go so far as to ask him for forever tonight, but she was going to ask for this.

When she let go of him, she knew he assumed it was because she was going to do what he'd just said and move to the bed. Instead, she picked up the silks she'd dropped to the floor when he'd been kissing her earlier. Still on her knees before him, she held them up and gave him one more chance.

"If I get on the bed, will you put these on me?"

No one had ever looked more conflicted than Rafe did in that moment, and she almost felt bad for him. Almost, but not quite. Because if he could only let go of his silly insistence on treating her "carefully"—along with his constant worries that he was going to hurt her in some way—she was certain that both of them would uncover something new. And spectacularly pleasurable.

Finally, with the muscle in his jaw jumping, he said, "I won't put those on you."

"Not even as a blindfold?"

Frustration lit his dark eyes, the same frustration he was making her feel with his stubborn belief that she was too sweet, too innocent for these kinds of sexy games.

"No."

"Okay," she said softly, "I just thought of a better use for them, anyway."

Sitting back on her heels, she lifted her hands to her hair. The thick strands were completely dry now, but still heavy as she gathered them up.

"Look," she added in a husky voice, "I can put them on all by myself."

She could see that he now realized she'd gotten off—and was about to get them both off—on a technicality. But it wasn't good enough for him to simply watch her wind the silks around her hair. She also needed him to know precisely *why* she was doing it.

"This way," she said softly as she tied the first knot in the soft fabric, "you'll have a really good view."

"View?" The one word from his beautiful mouth was strangled. Borderline desperate.

"Yes," Brooke replied, certain that he wanted this just as much as she did. In any case, he'd left her no choice but to take matters into her own hands—and mouth, too. A rush of heat hit her at the thought of what she was finally about to do. "Your view of me doing this."

A moment later he was on her tongue, and she was moaning from the pleasure of finally tasting his hard, hard flesh. He tasted so good that she found herself growing greedier with every inch of him she took inside her mouth. And, oh, how she loved it when he wrapped his hand in the silk binding around her hair to hold her just where he wanted her as he grew bigger, hotter, with every slick of her tongue.

Somehow, through the blood rushing in her ears, she heard him growling her name before he gave himself up completely to her mouth and her hands. She drank in his pleasure as if it were her own, and her lips would have curved up in a full smile if they weren't already wonderfully occupied.

A short while later, when he tugged at her silk-bound

ponytail and she rose to her feet, the ends of the silk were sticking to the damp skin between them.

"Promise me you'll never wear these in your hair again unless we're in the bedroom."

She made a show of considering his question. "Do you really think anyone else will know they aren't just pretty silk scarves?"

"I don't give a damn what anyone else knows. *I'd* know, damn it. *I'd* know what you did to me while you were wearing them in your hair. *I'd* know the way you actually smiled as I did that to you."

Of course, that made her smile even wider. "Can I help it if you make me happy?"

That light she was starting to see more and more sparked in the back of his eyes as he slid the silks from her hair.

"Promise me, or these go into the next bonfire."

"I promise I'll only wear them for you."

A split second later she was on the bed beneath him, and he was swearing he'd buy her more lingerie as he grabbed the lace and silk she was wearing and tore it off. She was thrilled by his rough, desperate possession, soon there were no more questions from either of them, no room for anything but sighs of pleasure and gasps of ecstasy as they wrapped themselves around each other.

But the most perfect moment of all came after they'd both toppled over the edge together, and he whispered the sweetest words she'd ever heard: "You make me happy, too."

Brooke was asleep within moments. Rafe loved the way she wrapped herself around him, her breathing even and soft now as she slept against his chest.

Every time they made love, she grew bolder, more confident in her ongoing quest to be wild. As he gently stroked her soft hair and breathed her in, he knew how frustrated she was that he kept refusing to do things like tie her up or blindfold her with the silks she'd brought home.

Didn't she realize that just the thought of having her arms bound to the bed frame and her eyes covered was cause for insanity? He was afraid it would be a slippery slope, especially when he was already so much rougher with her in bed than he'd ever intended to be. There were plenty of gentle moments between them, too, but the fact was, he'd lost it every single time. Holding down her wrists, shoving her up against the shower tiles, then taking her again on the bed inside of fifteen minutes.

He'd never forget the way she looked when she was down on her knees in that incredibly sexy outfit, her hair tied back so that he could see every beautiful expression on her face as she'd gazed up at him with the unabashed joy she brought to everything, including taking him into her mouth....

Damn it, he thought, as he buried his face in her sweet-smelling hair, he needed to stop replaying the sexy scene in his head or he'd end up being the most selfish bastard in the world by waking her up to take her again when she needed sleep to recover from her tiring day.

When she shifted against him, he wrapped his arms tighter around her, bringing her soft curves even closer. There was no point trying to deny that what they were doing had turned into so much more than just sex.

Rafe's chest clenched tight as he felt her breathe slow

and steady against his chest. The closer the two of them got, the more he worried about keeping her safe, not just with a dead bolt on her front door, but from people who would want to take advantage of her trusting, innately positive nature.

Brooke was so easy to be with that in moments like this, he could almost see himself spending the rest of his life with her. But could a cynic like him ever truly make her happy outside of the bedroom? And what would he do if the answer was no? Could he do the right thing and give up the one person who did the impossible?

Because when Brooke was in his arms, she made the darkness—and all the liars and the cheaters—disappear.

Nineteen

Holy crap, thought Rafe, as he looked in the delivery truck, his sister had bought a lot of furniture. And yet, once the crew finished unloading it all and placing it where Mia had indicated on the chart she'd made, Rafe had to admit it was exactly the right amount.

Brooke was next door taking care of the work she'd put aside to help him with his house. She'd lost another full day in Seattle yesterday, and he would have offered to help her make the chocolates for this week's upcoming delivery, but he figured he'd only end up getting in the way. Especially considering he couldn't be in the same room with her without ripping her clothes off and taking her.

As it was, he'd been hard-pressed to leave her bed that morning. There hadn't been one other thing he'd wanted more than to stay there, beneath the sheets, her warm curves pressed against him as he tasted and kissed and caressed every beautiful inch of her.

But since he'd known how much work she had to do, he'd forced himself to leave so that she could get to it.

There was still work to be done on his house, but as

he wandered through each of the fully furnished rooms, he couldn't deny that it was easily move-in ready. That first night, when he'd seen how trashed his family's old lake house had been, he'd been furious. He'd come to the lake to relax, not to renovate the place. But now, instead of being glad his house was perfectly habitable, down to the matching towels Mia had ordered for the bathrooms and the bookshelves in the living room that held new hardcover copies of his favorite authors, a hard knot fisted in his gut.

Until today, it had made perfect sense to stay with Brooke. But with a new bed, a clean bathroom and a decked-out kitchen, he could move into his own place now.

He should have been thrilled with the arrangement they'd made. Just sex. *Wild* sex, no less. It should have filled his independent male heart with glee that she'd clearly told him she wasn't looking to settle down, that she wasn't looking at him as her path to an engagement ring and a wedding dress.

Damn it, he wasn't thrilled with any of it.

And it didn't make a lick of sense that he wasn't.

Brooke had offered—hell, was offering it to him as often as he wanted, any way he wanted it—every guy's dream come true. A hot summer fling with no strings, with no expectations of anything but pleasure. But after only a handful of days with her in his arms, it wasn't enough.

It had only taken one night for the heat from their fling to quickly spiral into emotions deeper than he'd been expecting.

Then again, it wasn't really a few days or just one night, was it? He'd known Brooke a hell of a lot longer than any of the women he'd been with. As a kid, spending every summer next door to her for nearly ten years, at bonfires and waterskiing and hiking in the mountains together, he'd loved her the same way he loved his family. Because that's what she'd been and still was. Family.

But now? He'd be a liar if he didn't admit that the love he felt for her was a whole hell of a lot bigger. Stronger. And completely different from the love he had for his family or his other friends.

His cell phone rang, and though he wasn't in the mood to talk to anyone with his head and gut this twisted up, when he saw that it was Ben, he picked up. "You've found something?"

"Still putting things together," Ben said. "I've got a question for you."

Though Rafe wanted to push him, he knew Ben was adamant about triple-verifying everything before he would make an accusation. It was one of the reasons Rafe had been able to trust his colleague to keep the business running while he was here at the lake.

"Shoot."

"One name keeps coming up in association with Delacorte in the past six months. I wanted to check in with you about it, though, before I go any further. Do you know a Brooke Jansen?"

"She's my g—"

Damn it, she wasn't actually his girlfriend, was she? That wasn't in their summer-fling *agreement*.

Reminding himself that all Ben needed to do his job were the facts, Rafe told him, "We're next-door neighbors at the lake. I've been close to her since we were kids."

"Right," Ben said, clearly already knowing all of

that. "That's why I wanted to call before I went any further. Normally, since she's Delacorte's business partner, I'd do some digging into her details, as well."

Rafe had been so wrapped up in Brooke—and his concern about the possibility that she had partnered with someone who couldn't be trusted—that he hadn't thought things all the way through. Of course she would come up in the course of the investigation. If Rafe hadn't had a personal relationship with her, Ben would have simply done his job without asking questions. Instead, Rafe now had to make a judgment call about how to proceed.

At his prolonged silence, Ben finally asked, "Do you want me to investigate her, too?"

The word *no* was on the tip of Rafe's tongue. Brooke was an open book who looked at the rest of the world with trust shining from her pretty eyes. People with skeletons in their closets didn't smell like sunshine or laugh so often and so easily.

But how many times before had he been proved wrong? Especially during those early years of doing investigations when he didn't want to face up to what the real world actually looked like, what it was really made of.

He had to ask himself if the real reason he was reluctant to have Ben look more closely into Brooke's history and the details of her life was because he was afraid of what his employee would find. Because if Rafe really believed Brooke would come out of the investigation clean and pure and honest, then why would he stop Ben from completing the full investigation into her business partner, one that would have involved her in any case?

And, if he really was thinking along the lines of a

deeper, stronger love for her—something that sounded a hell of a lot like *forever*—shouldn't he be completely sure about everything she'd done between the ages of eight and twenty-six?

"Go ahead."

"With everything?" Ben asked, double-checking even this.

Rafe ignored the tightening in his gut as he confirmed, "Yes, everything," before they disconnected.

Having Ben do this background check on Brooke was the only way to be 100 percent sure.

And Rafe had never needed to be this sure about anyone before.

Brooke was knuckle-deep in chocolate ganache when her phone rang. She'd been waiting all afternoon for Cord to let her know how many boxes of truffles he needed for the press. Assuming it was him, she hit the speaker button on her phone with her cleanest finger and said hello.

"Hello, honey," her mother said in her crisp lawyer's voice. "Your father and I were hoping this would be a good time to finally discuss your new business venture."

Truffles in all stages were strewn across her kitchen counter. Brooke would likely have to work most of the night to pull off her deliveries for the week. But she wouldn't have given up the time she'd spent with Rafe for anything. A few missed hours of sleep were more than worth the incredible pleasure of being with him.

The sun burned hotter, the sky shone brighter, even the chocolate melting on her fingertips tasted richer now that Rafe had opened her eyes to the sensuality in everything around her.

Knowing that if she had time for Rafe she should also have time for her parents, she said, "Absolutely. How are you both?" as she continued hand-rolling truffles.

As always, she was amazed by the details of the groundbreaking legal case her mother had won, and her father's game-changing research on the economic effects of cell phones on developing countries. "Both of you are amazing," she told them, meaning every word. She was incredibly proud of her parents and their achievements.

"After your mother told me about your new partnership with my old colleague," her father said, "I gave Cord a call a short while ago."

She barely stifled her groan. She could only imagine the conversation the two of them had had, her father acting like she was still six years old and not to be trusted to cross the street by herself. "I hope the two of you had a nice conversation."

Thankfully, her father confirmed, "Indeed we did. He assured me that he has his eye closely on the ball and will make sure your new store in Seattle is a success."

While it had been exactly the right thing to tell her father, Brooke couldn't deny it grated that he was so quick to give Cord both the credit and the responsibility for the success of her business expansion. They still acted as if she'd been playing at her business these past years, rather than slowly growing her happy customer base month by month.

Trying to change the subject to something lighter, she said, "I hope you'll be able to come to our grand opening next month. Especially since we're having an absolutely beautiful summer here. You both should try to come out for a visit."

"Perhaps we could rearrange our schedules, although we wouldn't want to get in your way," her father said. "Is the house next door still a vacation rental?"

"Not anymore," she said, unable to keep the smile off her face. "The Sullivans bought it back just this week."

"The Sullivans have moved next door again?"

In the middle of carefully popping the lightly chilled truffles out of the molds and onto the counter, Brooke didn't catch the edge to her mother's question. "Well, Rafe is the one who bought the house, but since his sister and one of his brothers have already come up to visit this week, I'm sure the whole family will be using it quite a bit. They're all still very close."

"He must be married by now, surely?"

She frowned at the tone of her mother's question. "Rafe is only in his early thirties. He's not married. But he does own a very successful private investigation agency in Seattle."

"You sound like you know an awful lot about him after all these years, Brooke."

Though they couldn't see her over the phone, she lifted her chin in defiance. "We've spent quite a bit of time together since he bought the house. In fact," she added, in direct opposition to the voices in her head telling her not to, "he's been staying with me for the past week."

She could only imagine the coronaries they'd have if she added, *in my bed.* Her parents likely thought—or hoped, anyway—that she was still a virgin.

"Don't you have the common sense to know it isn't safe to let a man you barely know spend the night in your home? Haven't you learned anything at all since you snuck out of the house at sixteen, drank too much and got into that car with a boy who'd also been drinking?"

"I made one mistake ten years ago. *One!* But you keep bringing it up as if I've repeated it over and over every day since then." Hurt radiated from every word she spoke. "Why can't you trust me, and believe that I know what I'm doing, just once?"

"Why can't you be smart enough to say no when one of those wild Sullivans tells you he wants to spend the night in your home?"

"Because he's my friend." But she knew it would be dishonest to leave it at that. Her chin lifted yet another inch as she told them, "And more." Rafe Sullivan was the man she was falling head-over-heels in love with. She didn't want to hold it in anymore. "So much more."

"Oh, no," her mother said in obvious horror. "This was always what we were so worried would happen. We begged your grandparents to put some distance between you and that family and were so thankful when they had to sell the house. But now, after all these years, exactly what we feared has happened."

Brooke's hands fisted in chocolate as she stared at her phone. "How could you?" Her question was little louder than a hiss of pain. "They were like family, and you wanted to take them away from me? You were actually *glad* when they lost their house?"

But it was as if she hadn't spoken as her father said, "Even as teenagers, those Sullivan boys were dangerous. We always knew one of them would take advantage of the easy pickings next door."

Easy pickings?

My God, was that what her parents really thought she was? Just some naïve girl who couldn't think for herself? Who didn't have the strength of will—or enough common sense— to turn away a man she didn't want? Whom she didn't care for with every beat of her heart, and every last part of her soul?

But she already knew the answer to that, didn't she?

It was what her parents had always thought—that she was too fragile, too innocent, too foolish to know how to keep herself safe from harm. Only, now they'd pushed her too far.

It was one thing for them to think she wasn't capable of making good decisions. But to say that Rafe had pulled the wool over her eyes as if he was a dirty old man standing on the corner in a trench coat drawing her in with promises of candy?

That was what finally made her see red—and she addressed the comment in no uncertain terms.

"I'm the one who propositioned him." She barreled on despite her parents' shocked gasps. "He was trying to keep his distance, but I wouldn't let him. And being with him was the best decision I've ever made. Rafe Sullivan is the most wonderful man I've ever known. Better than any of the men you thought were so great, so safe. None of them cared about me the way he does."

Maybe he hadn't actually said he loved her, but that didn't mean she couldn't see how much he cared about her in every look he gave her, and feel it in every kiss, every time he was moving inside of her and making her soul take flight.

She heard Rafe's boots on her front porch and purposely said the one thing she knew would send her parents into even more of a tizzy. "Speak of the devil," she said with particular emphasis on the word *devil,* "he's just coming up the stairs now. I've got to go."

"Brooke—"

She didn't just hang up on them, she actually pulled the entire phone from the wall, leaving chocolate handprints on everything she touched.

"Thank God you're here," she said to Rafe when he stepped inside.

He was instantly worried. "What happened?"

She shook her head, reaching for him. "Nothing you can't fix." As he caught her up in his arms, she asked him, "How did you know I needed you right this second?"

"Because I need you, too. So damned bad that it nearly killed me to leave you alone so that you could get your work done."

"I don't want to be left alone." Not when he was everything she needed.

"Tell me what you do want, sweetheart."

"You." She pressed her mouth to the pulse point at the side of his neck. "Just you."

Twenty

Rafe lifted her up onto the kitchen counter so that she could wrap her arms and legs around him as he kissed her. "You taste so sweet."

"It's the chocolate."

"No, it's all you."

Her eyes filled up and her breath hitched in her lungs. Just as she'd told her parents, Rafe was different. Special. And he'd always noticed things more than other people.

To distract him from the questions she could see in his eyes—questions she didn't want to answer until she'd drawn strength from the beauty of their connection—she dipped her finger into the bowl of cooling ganache. "Taste this."

She knew she hadn't fooled him, but he was kind enough to let her sidetrack him as he lowered his mouth to her finger and licked it off.

"Do you like it?"

"I do," he said before he dipped his own finger into the bowl. Instead of feeding it to her, his mouth curved into the wicked smile she loved to see. "But I'm guessing it will taste even better like this."

He slowly slid his chocolate-covered finger across the upper curve of one breast above the neckline of her sundress. The anticipation of feeling his tongue in the same place held her breath captive in her lungs. Of course, he made her wait by tracing another strip of chocolate over the other side.

Finally, he lowered his head and slicked his tongue, warm and wet, over her skin. His shoulder muscles were hard beneath her hands as she held on to him for dear life. It was either that or go sliding off the counter in a puddle of liquid heat.

"I was wrong," he said after he'd licked up all of the chocolate.

The feel of his tongue on her bare skin, especially in the middle of the day in her kitchen while she had her legs wrapped around him, had turned her brain to mush. Somehow, she got her synapses to fire enough to ask, "You were?" even though she honestly couldn't remember what he could be wrong about.

"You taste so good that even the best chocolate in the world can't compare."

She'd been with men who, in months, hadn't made her feel as special as Rafe had in less than a week. She'd always been a little bit in love with him as a girl, had watched him be wild and free with stars in her eyes. But now she knew just how much more there was to him. He was a man who would do anything for his family. He was the P.I. who helped strangers with their problems by tracking down the answers they needed. And he was her lover who whispered the sweetest words she'd ever heard.

How could she do anything but fall all the way?

Brooke cupped his face in her hands and kissed him with all the love in her heart. But even though his kisses were pure magic, right now she needed more. She needed all of him, needed to feel him move inside of her and fill up all the spaces that the phone call with her parents had left empty.

She grabbed at his T-shirt so hard that it ripped as she yanked it up over his head. Her hands were at the fly of his jeans a heartbeat later and, thank God, he didn't try to stall her this time, wasn't planning to tease her today until she was begging.

He kicked off his shoes and jeans and boxers, and then he was lifting her hips off the counter enough that she could pull off her own dress. She was unhooking her bra when he reached for the lace between her legs and tore it from her body.

The thrill of being wanted, of being desired this much, shook through her. Completely naked now, she threw her arms and legs around him as he fisted his hands in her hair. Rafe tilted her head so that he could plunder her mouth in a sizzling kiss that told her exactly how he wanted her, hot and writhing beneath him, skin damp as she came again and again at his command.

The next thing she knew, he was pushing her bottom toward the center of the kitchen counter, and he was climbing up onto it with her. The granite was blessedly cool beneath her overheated skin, but Rafe's hands moving over every inch of her were more than enough to warm her again.

Both of them had slid into the chocolate by then and were covering each other's skin with it as they stroked and touched, licked and nibbled. What a thrill it was to have her two favorite things in the world at the same time: Rafe and chocolate.

She was just thinking how much easier it would be to never taste or make truffles again than it would be to lose Rafe when he sent all thoughts of loss from her head by moving fully between her thighs and driving into her in one perfect thrust.

"Oh God, Rafe."

Her words sounded as if they had come from a great distance rather than from her own lips. She was faintly aware of one of his large hands cradling her head while the other cupped her hip, protecting her from the granite, but she would have gladly gotten a few bruises. She didn't care about being safe, didn't care about anything but loving—and being loved—by the most beautiful man in the world. When they were together like this, nothing else mattered, only the joy that took her over from head to toe, inside and out.

She couldn't stop saying his name as he took her higher, and then higher still, and she finally realized he was saying her name, too, as their mouths found each other again in a heated kiss. Even caught up in desperation, they moved in perfect sync, from fast to slow and then back again. And when the wicked beauty of their lovemaking finally overwhelmed her, she arched back to take him even deeper as he held her tighter than he ever had before. Brooke had never felt more whole than she did as she came apart beneath him, his own release just moments behind hers.

It wasn't until he pulled away from her that she realized he must have taken out a condom before he'd dropped his jeans on the kitchen floor. She'd never been careless in bed with a man, had never truly lost control before Rafe, had never trusted anyone as much as she trusted him.

Yet again, he'd taken care of them both, just as she'd always known he would.

He lifted her from the counter and carried her into the bathroom, holding her tightly in his arms as he climbed into the tub and let the water pour in to wash the chocolate from both of them.

She leaned her head back against his shoulder and closed her eyes. "You're right. We don't need any props to be wild." She turned her face to his with a smile on her lips, but he wasn't smiling back. "You're not feeling guilty for debauching me again, are you?"

Clearly, he was surprised she'd figured him out so well. "I could have hurt you up on that hard granite."

"You could never hurt me."

She felt him stiffen behind her. Come to think of it, hadn't he looked a little twisted up about something when he walked into the kitchen? But she'd been so wrapped up in her own emotions that she hadn't stopped to ask if he was okay.

"Rafe?" She immediately twisted around in the tub so that she was straddling his hips, her hands linked around his neck. "We're not just lovers, we're friends, too. You can say anything to me. You know that, don't you?"

"I've never been friends with a lover before."

She caressed his cheek. "Me, either, but I think we're doing pretty good so far."

So good that she knew she couldn't expect him to be honest with her about what was on his mind if she wasn't honest with him, too. She could have avoided his earlier question again, the same way she had just minutes before. Especially when he was already hard again. Just the slightest shift of her hips and she could have both of them forgetting for a little while longer.

But for them to truly be more than lovers, even more than friends, meant talking not only about the cute things, the sexy things…but about the difficult things, too.

"You asked what happened when you walked into the kitchen." She sighed. "My parents called."

He slid a chocolate-covered strand of hair away from her forehead. "What did they say to upset you?"

"They still think I'm a little girl who needs their guidance, their protection, their wisdom. I'm not saying I don't want that sometimes, or that their learned wisdom isn't valuable, but—" She sighed, the water in the tub shifting beneath the slight movement of her body over his. "All these years I've been so sure that one day they'll open their eyes and see me. The real me, the woman I've become, not just a teenager who made a big mistake when she was sixteen. I can understand that they were terrified when I ended up in a car crash, but—"

"Wait a minute, what happened when you were sixteen?"

"I couldn't stand feeling like a prisoner in my bedroom another second, so when my friend suggested we sneak out to go to a party a couple of streets over, instead of saying no, like always, I said yes. But I had so little experience with regular teen stuff that when someone gave me a glass of punch, I drank all of it. And then another until the next thing I knew, everything was a little fuzzy."

"There was Everclear in that punch, wasn't there?

A hundred and ninety-proof alcohol with no taste, no smell."

She nodded. "I think so. But I probably would have been okay and made it back to my bedroom without my parents ever finding out if I hadn't gotten into a car with a boy I had a crush on." She winced. "He'd been drinking the punch, too, thus the crash into a tree in someone's front yard. The air bags caught me and I was fine, but—" She shook her head, feeling foolish about it even all these years later. "Pretty stupid, huh?"

"Yes, it was stupid," he agreed, and her heart started to sink just as he added, "but every teenager is stupid. Stupid is what teenagers do."

"Why can't my parents see that? Why can't they see me for who I am now? For who I've become?"

"I wish I could promise you that they'd come around," Rafe said softly, "but since I can't, all I can do is tell you what I see every time I look at you." His eyes were full of much more than desire as he caressed her cheek. "I see incredible beauty." He brushed the back of one hand down the curve of her body from breast to hip. "I see sensuality that shocks the hell out of me every single time we make love." He kept moving his hand down into the water until he'd picked up one of her hands. "I see the talent to make the best damned truffles in the world." He laid both of their hands between her breasts. "I see a heart that's big enough to take in my family showing up unannounced on your doorstep." He lifted her hand to his mouth and pressed a kiss to it. "But most of all, I see a woman who is so damned smart that she's done something few people will ever even realize they need to fight for—you've built your life exactly the way you want it, doing what you love, in the place you want to be. You don't need to prove one damned thing to anyone, Brooke. You already have."

With just a handful of the most beautiful sentences she'd ever heard, he'd answered every question she had left about falling in love with her next-door neighbor and friend, and had erased every last doubt.

All Brooke had ever wanted was for someone to actually see her—and to love her—for who she really was. Finally, she'd found him.

The first boy she'd ever loved would also be the last.

"Remember how I said that if you ever gave up being a P.I., you should consider short-order cooking?"

He cocked his head at her strange response to his incredibly sweet words. "You've got a hankering for eggs all of a sudden?"

"No, but I want you to know I've changed my mind. Plenty of people can make great scrambled eggs, but so few can be a poet."

"I'm no poet, Brooke."

"To me," she said as she laid her head against his shoulder, "you are."

Twenty-One

Rafe wanted to do anything he could to strip away the pain that lingered in Brooke's eyes after her phone call with her parents. But since more lovemaking would only put her more behind on her truffle-making schedule, he offered his two hands in whatever way she could use them to finish getting the rest of her orders made. She took him up on it with a big, happy smile that had him wasting a few more minutes of her tight deadline in his arms despite his best intentions to keep his hands off her until her work was done.

Earlier in the day, he'd been worried about being in her way, but as she quickly showed him what she needed him to do, he realized he should have given her enough credit to know exactly how to put him to work in such a way that he'd be a help rather than a hindrance.

He hated the thought of anyone harming her in any way. When he'd walked in after she'd gotten off the phone with her parents and she'd told him she'd needed him, he'd been desperate to heal the hurt in her eyes by replacing it with pleasure. Their lovemaking on the kitchen counter had been wild and hot, but more than that, it had been full of the sweetness that was at Brooke's core.

Everything she did held that same beautiful contradiction. The combination of heat and coolness in her chocolates. The simple sundresses over naughty lace and silk…or nothing at all. Wicked and oh so good. A man would be a fool not to look deeper than the surface with Brooke.

Did that mean he'd also been an even bigger fool about authorizing the background check on her?

And yet, even though Rafe had meant every word he'd said to her in the bathtub, though he'd seen with his own eyes her beauty, her brains and how big her heart was, what about all those years he hadn't been with her? Could there be something he needed to know that was bigger than sneaking out at sixteen and getting drunk, something she would never admit even to him? Something that would tear them apart down the road?

"Rafe?" He didn't realize he'd given voice to his frustration at the battle raging inside of him until she said his name. "You've already done so much to help. I'll come to bed after I've made my deliveries."

He moved from the boxes he was putting together to wrap his arms around her from behind. He rested his chin on the top of her head and loved the way she immediately relaxed back into his arms and chest. "I'm not going anywhere."

She turned her face to his, and he caught her lips in a soft kiss. Before she could spin around in his arms and convince him to ruin their hard work by lifting her up onto the counter to take her again in another rush of unquenchable desire, he moved his hands to her shoulders and began to give her a massage.

"*Oh, God.* Please don't stop doing that."

He grinned as he dug his fingers just a little harder into her muscles. "I'm glad it feels good."

"So, so good." Her eyes had closed and her head fell forward as she let herself enjoy every second of the impromptu massage. "A short-order cook, a poet, and now a masseur. You're so good at everything you do."

He pressed a kiss to her head. "You must inspire greatness in me."

She rubbed her hips against his groin. "I wonder what else I can inspire?"

"As soon as we get the rest of these chocolates made and out the door, we can find out," he promised her, before reluctantly lifting his hands and stepping away from her gorgeous, extremely inspiring curves to get back to work on filling truffle boxes.

The sky was dark, the moon only a sliver now. As they worked, its reflection on the surface of the water outside moved across the lake until it was replaced by the rising sun.

"No doubt about it," she said as they put together the last handful of boxes, "I'm officially too old for all-nighters. Thank you for helping. I couldn't have even come close to pulling this off without you."

"You wouldn't have been this far behind without me, either."

"We're having another one of our silly arguments again," she said with a little smile. "Come on and let's get these delivered so that we can get back to being in-spired, instead."

People were going to wonder—and assume—when they saw him with Brooke this morning. It was a small, tight-knit town. He hadn't been a part of it for the past eighteen years, but he hadn't forgotten how it worked. Word had likely spread like wildfire that he'd bought the lake house his family used to own, and he doubted his dinner or motorcycle ride with Brooke had gone unnoticed, either.

The locals would wonder how on earth he'd gotten to be the luckiest bastard on the planet. But more than that, they'd want to know if he was even close to good enough for one of their own.

They were the exact two things Rafe kept wondering himself.

Four hours later, Brooke was asleep in the passenger seat as he drove her car back up the long gravel driveway lined with Douglas firs that led to both their houses. They'd driven to the main shopping areas of the three towns closest to the lake and delivered chocolates to every gift store, grocery, sweet shop and ice cream stand. He'd been momentarily surprised when Brooke stopped in at the police and fire stations with free boxes of chocolate. It was a brilliant marketing idea, and he'd seen the incredible goodwill everyone in town had for her, but that wasn't why she did it. She simply wanted to show her appreciation for the difficult and important work the cops and firefighters did.

He'd run into guys at the stations he hadn't seen in years, and while they'd clearly been glad to see him again, he'd also felt the weight of their silent warning: *Screw around with Brooke and you're screwing around with all of us.* On top of that, more than one of them had clearly been upset that he'd stolen the prettiest girl in town out from under their noses. Knowing just how many guys would have been more than willing to be "wild" with her had Rafe feeling even more possessive and protective of her.

His sister had been right: Summer flings never worked out the way they were supposed to. Maybe, he found himself thinking as he unbuckled Brooke's seat belt then lifted her out of the car, that was because sometimes they worked out even better.

She nuzzled her face into his neck as he carried her inside. Laying her down on her bed, he intended to gently strip her clothes off without waking her up, but she wouldn't let go of him.

"It's time to be inspired."

Her whispered words in his ear had him growing even harder than he'd been just from holding her in his arms. She inspired not only deep desire, but also emotions he would have been on guard against with anyone but her.

Brooke had slipped in beneath his defenses, not just with sweet kisses and incredibly hot lovemaking, but with her constant smiles and laughter that jumped like a cannonball into the dark spots inside of him and splashed them with light.

"I'm always inspired when I'm with you."

Her eyes fluttered up, arousal quickly edging out the sleepiness. "Show me."

Her mouth was so damned soft, her tongue so sweet, that all he could manage to show her was the fact that he couldn't resist her.

Every time they'd made love had been special. Perfect. Wild. This was their first time for sleepy and slow, her body like melting butter beneath his.

How many other ways would there be to love her?

It was a question he knew he'd enjoy trying to answer every day for the rest of his life.

Her skin smelled like chocolate, and he breathed her in all over as he slowly stripped her clothes away and ran kisses from her temple down to the brightly painted tips of her toes. She stretched like a contented, sleepy kitten beneath his increasingly heated caresses, purring like one, too, every time he found a particularly sensitive spot with his tongue.

He could have spent the rest of the day tasting behind her knee, nipping at her hipbone, rubbing his cheek against the undersides of her breasts, but there were so many other spots he needed to taste, too.

The soft skin on her neck when she arched beneath him.

The small of her back when he rolled her onto her stomach so that he could fully appreciate the gorgeous curve of her hips while massaging away the aches that came with doing such hard work at the kitchen counter all night long.

The shadow of curls between her thighs that tempted a man beyond reason.

She was pliant enough in her drowsy passion that he could easily turn her in his arms and open her thighs with his as he took care of protection. And then she was reaching for him again, and her mouth was connecting with his at the exact moment he slid into her. She was so wet and hot and ready for him that he nearly lost it right then and there.

Cheek to cheek as they moved together, he could tell by the way her inner muscles clenched around him that she was as close as he was. Sex for Rafe had always been a marathon, a test to see how far he could push his partner and himself. But with Brooke there were no goals, no rules, no awards he was trying to win. Just pleasure.

And pure joy.

He could feel her mouth curve up against his cheek as she approached her climax. Only this time, as he increased his thrusts to help take her all the way over the edge, she gave him more than her smile, more than the sweet sound of her laughter.

"I love you."

Her mouth was so close to his ear as she gave him her heart that he almost felt as though the words had always been there inside his head, flipping every off switch to on, turning every red light to green.

Rafe knew Brooke hadn't said the three little words to try to get him to say them back, or to push him into making a decision he wasn't yet ready for. She'd simply given him what was inside her heart, just as she'd given him her body.

And in that instant, Rafe knew it didn't matter what Ben's background check said. Brooke could have a thousand skeletons in her closet and he'd still love her.

"I love you, too."

He swore time stopped as her eyes opened. She looked up at him in stunned surprise. "You do?"

All these years he'd been so certain love only happened once in a blue moon, but somehow they'd gotten one, hadn't they?

"I do, so damned much. You're all I can think of, all that I'm going to want forever."

Her eyes filled with tears even as a wide smile split her face. Just as she laughed through every orgasm, she did the same now while teardrops rolled down her cheeks. After he kissed each of them away, she whispered one word against his mouth.

"Forever."

Twenty-Two

A ringing cell phone woke them up. Rafe pulled Brooke closer, intent on ignoring anything that wasn't warm and soft and smelling like chocolate in his arms, but the damned thing kept buzzing again and again.

She finally murmured against his shoulder, "Sounds like it's pretty important."

By the fifth time it rang, he'd begun to think the same thing. Worried that something had happened to his siblings or his parents, he kissed Brooke on the forehead, then eased out of her bed. Through the window, he could see that the sun was high in the sky, and her bedside clock said it was past noon. They hadn't slept more than a handful of hours after working all night long, but every hour in bed with Brooke was worth at least two without her.

She loved him.

The memory of the way she'd said those three incredible words to him just hours ago—and how he'd, amazingly, said them right back—had him wanting to toss his phone out into the lake so that the two of them could be left alone in their cozy little world together.

He grabbed his jeans from the chair in the corner of Brooke's bedroom, and his cell fell onto the carpet. Ben's name staring up at him from the screen froze Rafe in place. If there hadn't been anything of note to report, his colleague would have sent an email or left a voice mail.

Clearly, five calls in a row meant Ben needed to reach Rafe immediately.

"Rafe?" Brooke was sitting up in bed now, the covers bunched up around her waist, her hair tangled from their lovemaking. "Is it your family? Is everything okay?"

"It's the office. I'll take the call out in the living room so that you can get back to sleep." Before he left, he gave her one more lingering kiss, one that stunned him all over again with its sweetness.

Her eyes were hazy with more than sleepiness by the time he made himself move away from the bed. He yanked on his jeans and closed the bedroom door behind him.

His gut twisted tight as he dialed Ben back. Was this how his clients felt when they saw his name come up on their phones, calling with the bad news they'd been praying he wouldn't give them? He'd always tried to be sensitive about it, but now he wondered if he'd ever been anywhere close to sensitive enough.

When Ben picked up, Rafe said, "I want to know what you've got on Delacorte, but—" he lowered his voice and moved farther from the bedroom "——I already know everything I need to know about Brooke. You can shred whatever you've got on her."

He knew now that there wasn't a damn thing she could have done to make him stop loving her. He'd been crazy to tell Ben to do a background on her in the first place, almost as if he'd been looking for a way to sabotage his own happiness.

"I've already emailed you the document I put together, so if you don't want to read the background on Brooke, you should skip page ten," Ben told him. "I'll take care of destroying the hard copies here."

"Good. Now tell me what you found on her partner."

Ben quickly outlined the details of what he'd learned about Cord Delacorte. Rafe cursed. It wasn't good. He badly wanted to get on his Ducati, blast into Seattle and tear the guy's heart out with his bare hands. Later, Rafe promised himself, he'd do exactly that. But first he'd need to give Brooke the bad news, and console her over it.

After thanking his colleague for doing excellent work, there was one more thing Rafe needed to take care of. "I want you to become a full partner in the firm, Ben. How does that sound to you?"

"Good. Really good."

"I do have one condition, though, and it's an important one." It was funny how clear it all was now. "I don't want us investigating any more cheaters. I know it's a huge part of our business and we do help people who need it, but I think it's time we let our competitors in on those cases."

"You've got my complete agreement on that," Ben said, and then, "Getting away for a while has been good, hasn't it?"

Getting away had definitely been good, but falling in love with Brooke had been what made him see things in a new light. Light he hadn't been able to see in a very long time.

"Everything's going well here. No rush coming back, boss."

"Partner," he reminded Ben with a grin as he hung up.

Unfortunately, his smile fell away as soon as he downloaded the information Ben had emailed onto his cell phone. Rafe had just finished reading through the first nine pages when Brooke emerged from the bedroom.

She was gorgeous in a silky blue robe that barely skimmed her thighs. "You should still be in bed sleeping," he told her.

Of course, he loved the way she walked straight into his arms and lifted her mouth to his for a kiss. It would be so easy to celebrate what they'd found with each other and forget for a little while longer what Ben had told him about her business partner. But Rafe didn't want any darkness in her life at all, which meant he needed her to know what was going on. As soon as he reassured her that everything was going to be okay, he would head out to rectify the situation with her soon-to-be ex-partner. And he wouldn't feel the least bit bad about using his fists for at least part of the "rectifying."

"As soon as you left the room, Cord called," she told him, and he realized she had her own phone in her hand. "Looks like I'll need to head back into Seattle today for what is evidently a really important last-minute meeting with the neighborhood retail association. Is everything okay at your office? Do they need you back in the city today, too?"

It was hard to keep his fury in check as he sat on the couch with her cradled on his lap, stroking her cheek with the back of one hand. "Actually, your partner is the reason my colleague Ben called." Knowing it was best just to spit it out, he said, "I'm sorry to have to tell you this, but Cord is stealing from you."

She blinked at Rafe with that look of shock on her face that made him hate days like this in the office so much. God, he hated giving bad news to people. Especially to a woman like Brooke, who saw the good in everyone and everything.

He prayed this one incident wouldn't steal away her optimism.

Her soft hair floated around her shoulders and breasts as she shook her head in confusion. "I don't understand what makes you think Cord is stealing from me."

Just hearing her partner's name made Rafe's hands curl into fists. He wanted to take out his fury with every cheating, scheming, stealing asshole in the world on the guy's too-pretty face.

"As soon as we started spending time together and you told me about your new business partnership, even knowing you must have done your own background checks on the guy, I did one, too. That way, if there were any red flags, you could get out before you were pulled in too deep. Unfortunately, my team found one hell of a red flag."

Shock mingled with deep disappointment in her beautiful eyes. "You investigated Cord?"

Rafe suddenly felt like he was fumbling. Instead of being angry with Delacorte, she seemed upset with *him*.

"He withdrew money from the trust account your grandparents set up for you—the one you've barely touched since they passed away—and used it to pay for an extremely expensive fertility treatment. I'm absolutely certain their doctor will immediately refund the money as soon as we inform them of what happened."

"I don't want the fertility clinic to refund my money." By the time she'd finished her sentence, she was off his lap and standing in the middle of the living room staring at him as if she'd never seen him before.

Rafe stood, too. "I know he took you in, convinced you he's someone he's not. But he stole from you, and you're going to get every penny back from him and then some."

"No," she said with a firm shake of her head, "*he's* not the one who convinced me he's someone he isn't." Her words had a horribly ominous tone. "At this point, I'm not even sure you deserve to hear the truth, but if I don't tell you, I'm guessing you'll just keep poking around in everyone's background without permission until you can find a way to prove that you're right."

"I've just told you the truth, Brooke."

"No," she said in a harder voice than he ever thought he'd hear from her, "you've just given me your sneaky, twisted, cynical version of what happened." She turned her face away as if she couldn't stand to look at him. "After our meetings in Seattle were through this week, I asked Cord and his wife to have a quick drink with me. Despite everything going well with our business, I could tell how down he was, and it wasn't hard to guess why. Their fertility doctor had just told them they had one more round of IVF left before it was time to give up trying to have a baby, but it had to be done right away or the clock would have run down too far for his wife, who is several years older than he is. They've already run through their available cash, and the rest is tied up in our business. I told them I wanted to help, but they wouldn't take my money. But because we're friends—real friends who talk about our feelings and dreams—I know how badly they want to have a baby and how hard it's been on them to fail to conceive. I gave his doctor my trust account information for direct billing. That way, the money was already spent, and he and his wife, who is also now a friend of mine, had to take it."

Fuck. He couldn't believe how badly he'd gotten things wrong. And yet, she had to understand why he'd done it, didn't she?

"I can't tell you how glad I am to hear that he wasn't stealing from you, but…"

The rest of his sentence fell away as he looked into her eyes and finally realized what heartbreak—and betrayal—looked like.

"Can't you see that by checking up on my business partner like this, especially after I'd already told you that I'd done my research, you've treated me exactly like my parents always have—as if I'm not capable of making savvy business decisions? How could you, Rafe? Especially when you just told me last night that you see the real me."

"I *do* see you," he swore to her. "But you don't know what else I've seen. Not just men cheating on their wives. Not just wives cheating on their husbands. But people planning horrible things. Extortion. Blackmail. Kidnappings. And worse. You have no idea what people are capable of, but I know exactly what could have been in that report Ben emailed me. Can't you understand, Brooke? I needed to be sure. Completely sure."

Brooke felt everything that wasn't already breaking inside of her begin to shatter at his words.

"I needed to be sure."

"What else did you need to be sure about?" she asked in a soft voice. "Just my business decisions…or me, too?"

He reached for her. "Brooke—"

She took one step away from him, and then another. "I get that you don't trust people. I even mostly understand your reasons. That's why I said you could ask me anything. *Anything.* But instead of asking me what you wanted to know about my past—" She worked to stay strong enough, steady enough, but she had to ask. "Did you do a background check on me?"

Unfortunately, she could read the answer on his face even before he said, "I swear I haven't read it and I'm not going to."

Suddenly, she could hardly breathe. But it wasn't the wonderful kind of breathlessness that took her over when he was kissing her. No, this was a horrible, terrible pain that resonated deep in her chest.

"It was one thing for you to investigate Cord, and I can almost forgive you for thinking that being overprotective means you're taking care of me. But how could you possibly justify running a background check on me? Don't you know me at all after the past week? Or how about after we practically grew up together?" He'd just told her he loved her for the first time hours ago. But how could he love her if he'd done this? "You told me you would never forgive yourself if we slept together in the heat of the moment and I woke up the next morning and decided it was a mistake. But I *knew* that would *never* happen. Because you could never be a mistake." The pain beneath her breastbone intensified as she said, "I can't believe I was wrong."

"You're not wrong, Brooke. I'm not a mistake. *We're* not a mistake." He started to reach for her again, but when she flinched, he dropped his hand. "I'm sure about loving you. Absolutely, one hundred percent sure. I think I always was, right from the start, but with everything moving so fast it was easier to tell myself that I didn't know where my head was than to admit that I had fallen in love with you this fast. This hard. This deep." His breath came fast, as if he'd been running a race. "I know I screwed up big-time with this report—"

"I want to see it." It would be so easy to let herself listen only to his words of love, of how deeply he claimed to feel it. She forced herself to focus on what he'd done, instead. "I want to see what you found out about me in your background check."

"Brooke—"

"Show it to me, Rafe."

His eyes were wary as he reluctantly handed her his phone. "Ben told me it's on page ten so that I could skip it."

As she scrolled through the report and quickly read through the list of all of her old addresses, her previous jobs, information about her parents and their jobs, one stupid tear fell onto the screen, and she dashed it away with the back of her hand.

"You missed the candy bar I slipped into my bag at the corner store when I was five because my parents wouldn't buy it for me."

"Brooke—"

She scowled at the man who had made her cry out with pleasure mere minutes before…and who now was just making her cry. "And there's the math test where I copied an answer from the girl sitting next to me when

I was ten because I ran out of time and panicked about not bringing home an A. You should make sure you have your staff add that to the reports for the next guy who decides he has to do a background check before he can decide whether he's *sure* enough to let himself love me."

"I was an idiot for not trusting you," he said in a voice made raw with emotion, and something that sounded like fear. "I was a fool for thinking you might have skeletons in your closet like everyone else."

"But I do have them, Rafe. I'm not perfect. Nobody is. And if you'd asked me about my past instead of running this stupid report, I would have told you that my parents told me over and over my whole life to be careful, to watch out, to make sure I didn't get hurt. I would have told you that my grandparents taught me to believe in myself, and in others, but that no matter how hard I try I haven't been able to completely shake away the fear my parents instilled in me. Not until you. I would have told you that I knew I would be safe being wild with you because you would never let anything bad happen to me." She didn't bother to wipe her tears away this time, not when she knew more would just fall. "And I would have told you that finding out you'd bought the house next door felt like my birthday and Christmas all wrapped up into one, because you hadn't just come back to the lake. You'd come back to *me*. I saw that you were darker, more cynical, but I thought I could help erase your pain with fun and laughter. And love. But now—" Her breath shook, along with her limbs. "Now I don't know what to think."

"You did help." Didn't she see? "You showed me I could love when I didn't think it was possible." Rafe wanted to reach for her so badly that his fingers were actually cramping from holding them in check. But she hadn't offered him another touch, and he sure as hell hadn't earned it yet. "I can change. I swear I can, for you." Feeling as if he was grasping at straws, he told her, "I just told Ben that we're not going to take infidelity cases anymore. I don't want to see any more relationships fall apart, and I don't want any of my employees to have to deal with seeing it, either."

"I'm glad to hear that," Brooke said softly, but she was too pale and looked terribly fragile. "But I don't know if that changes the fact that I always trust, even when I shouldn't. And you always doubt, even when you shouldn't. I wanted to believe we could make this work, that we could love each other through the rough patches, but—"

"We can. We will. Let me start by loving you right, Brooke. Let me prove to you I can fix everything I broke. Let me start replacing doubt with trust."

"Maybe my parents are right," she said softly. "Maybe I don't know how to make good decisions. Because even though I know I should be kicking you out after what you've done, I just can't."

She could have told him to get the hell out of her house, then rammed the dead bolt home to keep him out. But even though he'd hurt her, badly, he could still see the love in her beautiful eyes. She'd never been able to hide that from him.

"Thank God," he said, relief sweeping through him as he reached for her.

For one perfect heartbeat she let him hold her…but then she slid out of his arms and moved far enough away that he couldn't reach out and touch her again.

•

"That day on the beach when we first kissed, you said we needed twenty-four hours to make sure we thought things through. While I'm in Seattle for the next twenty-four hours, we both need to do some more thinking. At least," she added with an exhausted sigh, "I do."

"You're not coming home tonight?"

Her eyes flashed with surprise at the way he'd called this *home.* Though he'd lived in Seattle his whole adult life, he'd never felt as though he was truly home until he'd shared one with her.

"I can't think straight when I'm with you, Rafe." The breath she took shook through her. "I need to be sure. Completely sure."

God, he hated hearing his own words coming back at him. Hated even more knowing what a fool he'd been to ever think them in the first place. Desperation clawed at him to get her back…and to make her stay.

He knew if he kissed her the way he had that first afternoon out on the beach when both of them were dripping wet, he could keep her from leaving, he could get her to change her mind about taking twenty-four hours to think about whether they could make things work.

But Rafe had already made too many mistakes with Brooke. Using their attraction in an attempt to temporarily bind her to him would only destroy whatever was left of the love she still had for him.

So when she said, "I need to get ready to leave now," then turned to walk back into her bedroom and closed the door behind her with a soft click, even though it nearly destroyed him, he let her go.

Twenty-four hours.

He had twenty-four hours to figure out how to prove

to her that he could change…and that he could love her the way she deserved to be loved.

Brooke stood in her bedroom and stared at her unmade bed where Rafe had made such sweet love to her hours ago…and where she'd told him she loved him. She hadn't had a single doubt. Hadn't had a single fear. She'd simply given him her heart with the perfect certainty that he'd never harm it.

As a child, Brooke had looked at Rafe Sullivan with stars in her eyes. Eighteen years later, when he'd touched her as a woman, those stars had transformed into something so bright, so beautiful, that she'd been blind to anything else. All she'd wanted for him was to see him smile more easily, more often. And for herself she wanted a little taste of being wild and safe and warm in his strong arms.

She'd loved him so much that she'd believed she had enough faith in the world for both of them, enough to help renew his faith in people, to show him that love could change everything.

But could it?

Twenty-Three

It had been barely fifteen minutes since Brooke had driven away, yet Rafe missed her so badly already that he'd almost fired up his motorcycle a dozen times to race after her. But she'd given him twenty-four hours when he'd asked for it. He owed her the same, owed her one more chance to think things through.

He had left Seattle for the summer to get away from the assholes for a little while so that he could clear his head…only to find out that he was the real asshole. And now, if he couldn't convince her to take him back, he'd have to come to the lake every summer, wave at her from his porch next door, and watch her fall in love with some other guy who was smart enough to know a good thing when he held it in his arms. It would kill Rafe to see Brooke grow pregnant with another man's children, and to have someone else teach them to swim and tell them scary stories around the bonfire at night, all the while knowing that that guy should have been *him*.

But he'd been so stuck on focusing on everything bad in the world that he hadn't let himself see that the very best thing had been in his arms the whole time.

He was supposed to be a great investigator, but he'd ignored every loving, honest cue Brooke had given him.

Although Rafe now had a newly renovated and furnished home, a home that had once been filled with the love and laughter of his family, he finally understood where his real home was. With Brooke.

A week ago, next door hadn't seemed like far enough away in case things went wrong with their fling. But now it was too far away. He couldn't stay here, couldn't imagine spending even one night in his new bed without her curled up against him.

God, he was such an idiot. He'd been so worried about hurting Brooke, about stripping away her innocence with kinky sex. But nothing they'd done in the bedroom had taken away the sweet light in her eyes. No, sending Ben out to dig into her past had been what had finally torn the veil away.

Her parents had never let themselves see the real Brooke, and he'd told her he had. But he'd been so scared about what he'd seen whenever he looked into her eyes that he'd tried to look through the cynical investigator's eyes instead of those of a man who had fallen in love fast and hard. He'd come up with the perfect way to test that forever…and to make sure she knew exactly how far he was from being a man she could count on to share her sunny, sweet life.

And all the while he'd believed that it was better to throw something away than to have it stolen from him later.

Rafe hadn't cheated on Brooke, but it was just as bad that he hadn't talked to her, or had enough respect for her strength to tell her how scared he was about loving her, and about whether he could be the man she needed him to be. He'd been so proud of himself for never cheating on a woman, when all the while it turned out that he was worse than any of the scum he'd caught cheating over the years.

How was he going to fix things?

These were the most important twenty-four hours of his life, and he felt lost. Completely, utterly lost. He'd finally put a stop to the investigations that had darkened his heart, but was it too little, too late?

Other people came to Rafe Sullivan for help. He didn't go to them. But, suddenly, he realized he'd been a fool for more than one reason, with more than just Brooke. His family had always been there for him, but he'd shut them out. Not just after he'd been slashed with the knife, but long before that, when his job—and life— had become something he didn't much like anymore.

He pulled the phone out of his pocket and dialed. "Mia, I need your help."

"Rafe? What happened?" Of course, before he could answer, his sister had already guessed it had something to do with Brooke. "What did you do?"

"I screwed everything up, just like you predicted."

"How?"

"I ran a background check on Brooke's business partner without checking with her first."

She paused a moment before replying, "Well, that shows a major lack of respect, but honestly, even though I'm sure she's mad about it, I don't think it's anything you can't come back from if you grovel enough."

"That's not all, Mia." He swallowed hard at the full extent of his stupidity. "I did a background on Brooke, too."

"Oh, shit, Rafe." She was silent for a long moment

and Rafe steeled himself for her next comment. "You're my brother, and I love you, but you sure aren't making it easy on a sister to help. Because if a man I was sleeping with did that to me—"

"We aren't just sleeping together. I love her. And I only have twenty-four hours to figure out a way to get her back."

He didn't know what he expected Mia to say to him upon hearing that he'd fallen in love with her childhood friend. He only knew it wasn't, "You would never have done something like that if you didn't love her." Of course Mia followed it up with something he *did* expect. "I swear, men are so stupid sometimes I can't believe there's any of you left."

She let out a long, deep sigh. "If you had just forgotten her birthday or something like that, I could give you an easy fix. You know, a dozen roses or standing outside her window while you recite the poetry you wrote about how beautiful she is. But after what you've done, I'm going to need some time to think of a much better way for you to unlock her heart again so that she can trust you."

"Unlocking her heart," he said slowly as the first answer came to him in a rush. "Thanks for being there for me, sis."

"Wait a minute, I haven't even told you what to do yet."

"Just wish me luck." As soon as she did, Rafe shoved the phone in his pocket and headed straight for his motorcycle.

Maybe, the cynical voice inside him cautioned as he rode toward the hardware store, his plans to unlock Brooke's heart wouldn't be enough to win her back.

And maybe a day, a week, a year ago, he never would have tried.

But not today. Not when he was finally willing to believe that there was a chance to reclaim the love he'd stupidly compromised.

He'd grovel. He'd beg. He'd plead. He'd strip off every last layer of pride to try to win back Brooke's love. He'd make sure to undo each of his mistakes, one by one, during the next twenty-four hours.

And then, if that failed, he'd start all over again at the beginning.

Brooke felt as though she'd been sleepwalking through her meetings in Seattle. Cord had expressed concern about how pale she was when she first arrived, but she knew if she let down her guard for even one second, she wouldn't be able to reclaim it. The last thing she wanted was to meet everyone in the local retail association with eyes red from crying, and cheeks wet with tears, so she made sure to hold it together all day long.

When she'd come alone to Seattle just two days earlier it had been less to think through things with Rafe than to drop into Indulgence to purchase a few sexy surprises for him. But this time, all there was ahead of her for the next twenty-four hours were swirling thoughts and questions.

The only thing she knew for sure was how much she loved Rafe.

If only she knew whether or not that love would be enough....

At the end of the day, after turning down Cord's offer to take her for a drink, she headed on foot through the city. The sky was heavy with the threat of rain, and she found herself hoping it would start to pour, that maybe the rain could wash away her doubts. Doubts she'd never allowed herself to feel before today.

As she walked down the sidewalk, every man she saw with dark hair and broad shoulders had her hoping it was Rafe and that he'd ignored her request for twenty-four hours apart.

Brooke sighed at her wildly careening emotions. When he'd told her he wanted to make up for what he'd done, every cell in her body had wanted to lean back into him and stay right there in the circle of his arms. It had been the hardest thing she'd ever done to force herself to be smart…and to leave to put some thinking space between them.

She was resilient. She was strong. But if things stayed the way they were, how long would it be until her love for him finally shattered one too many times? And yet, hadn't he already made a step in the right direction by changing the focus of his investigations away from broken marriages?

Brooke thought she must be hallucinating when she looked up just then and saw the name Sullivan on the large sign right above where she was standing. My God, she was a mess, not only seeing Rafe in every stranger on the street, but seeing his name on every sign, too.

Right then, as if on cue, the sky finally opened up. Brooke wiped a hand over her eyes to try to clear the rain from her vision, and had just realized the sign said Sullivan Realty, when she heard her name.

"Brooke?" Mia was clearly surprised to see her. "What are you doing here in the rain in front of my office?"

Before Brooke could reply, Mia took her hand and

pulled her inside the building. The next thing Brooke knew, she was sitting on a plush leather couch in a large corner office with a hot cup of coffee in her hands. And as she turned to look at her friend, who was sitting beside her on the couch looking extremely worried, it was as if the rain had washed away her inner filters.

"I thought I could heal Rafe," Brooke blurted out, each word etched with the pain she had worked so hard to hold at bay all day long. "I thought I could love him enough to make the darkness go away. But what if I can't?"

She couldn't tell if the wetness on her cheeks was from her tears or from the rain, but it didn't matter as her friend took the untouched coffee from her hands, put it down on the glass table in front of them and folded her into her arms.

Mia was a small woman, but her arms were warm and strong. Just like her brother's were.

A few minutes later, Mia handed her a box of tissues, and once she'd dried her face, she handed her the coffee. It was hot and black, and after the long cry, Brooke finally felt a little bit steadier as she sipped it.

"Rafe called me this morning," Mia said softly.

Brooke nearly dropped the mug. She put it back down on the table so she didn't spill the hot coffee. "Is he okay?"

Mia was clearly surprised by her question. "If he'd done to me what he did to you, that definitely wouldn't be my first concern." She cocked her head. "You really do love my brother, don't you?"

Brooke's brain felt clogged from her recent cry, and from missing Rafe so badly during the past eight hours. "You know I do. I always have."

"Thank God," Mia said, "because he called to ask me to help him figure out how to win you back." Brooke could feel the ice inside her chest begin to melt as Mia told her, "And even though he seemed to figure out the answer for himself before I could come up with something, it was still a really big deal that he actually called. Because I honestly can't think of the last time he asked me for help. Or any of us. Rafe thought it was his job to help us and everyone else, rather than it ever being the other way around."

"It's why he's a P.I.," Brooke murmured. "So that he can help people out of the darkness."

"We've all tried to reach out to him over the years, and even though I was able to convince him to take some time off to go to the lake this summer, none of us came close to helping him during the past few years the way you've done in less than a week, Brooke. We all love Rafe, but *your* love is what made the difference, not ours."

Mia, Brooke suddenly realized, was a secret romantic. One who had clearly been hurt, but who still, in her inner heart of hearts, believed in love.

True love.

The same love that Brooke had felt for Rafe from the start.

The same love she felt for him right now.

Yes, it hurt that Rafe hadn't trusted her enough to treat her like the friend she was supposed to be. Hurt like hell, actually, going deeper than any pain she'd ever known. But hadn't she known that Rafe had his own deep scars, bigger ones on the inside than the one slashed across his ribs by an angry ex-husband?

After what he'd seen as an investigator, it made sense

that he'd been afraid to believe true love was real, or that it could last.

Of course he'd try to prove himself right…and she'd almost let him do just that by walking away from him after he'd made his mistake.

Brooke gave Mia a quick hug before hopping up off the couch. "Thank you. For everything. I've got to go. He needs me."

Brooke shot out of the door and was heading back up the rainy sidewalk before Mia could even say goodbye. For the second time in one day, Mia hadn't gotten a chance to tell either her brother or Brooke what to do after they'd come to her for support.

Clearly, Mia thought with a smile as she sat down behind her computer for another late night in the office, Rafe and Brooke were meant to be together.

Twenty-Four

Three hours later

"Brooke?" Rafe rubbed his hand over his eyes as if he was afraid she was a figment of his imagination instead of standing right in front of him. "It hasn't been twenty-four hours yet."

My God, he was beautiful. Strong. Loving. And a little bit broken, just like everybody else.

Her heart racing, Brooke told him, "I couldn't stay away from you another minute."

She wasn't just in his arms a moment later…she was finally home. They might still have a long road to go with each other, but from here on out, they'd travel that road together. And she'd never make the mistake of walking away from him again, no matter what mistakes they'd inevitably make with each other along the way.

"I love you." He whispered the words again and again into her hair. "I love you so much."

She was lifting her face from his chest to tell him she loved him, too, when she realized her grandmother's recipe book was lying on the table in her grandfather's workshop. She'd been so worried when she'd returned at 10:00 p.m. and Rafe hadn't been in either house that when she'd seen the light through the trees, she hadn't walked along the path to the workshop, she'd run as fast as her legs could carry her.

Her hands were shaking as she reached for her grandmother's recipe book. "It's fixed." She looked up at the beautiful man she'd loved her whole life. "You fixed the broken heart."

Brooke ran trembling fingers over the wooden cover, which looked as perfect as it had the first time she'd seen it as a little girl. There was no crack anymore, not even the slightest sign that the heart had ever been split in two. She pressed her palm over the heart, and when she closed her eyes, she swore she could feel her grandfather and grandmother with them in that moment.

Oh, how happy they would have been to see her and Rafe together, and to know that there would be many, many more summers of love between the Sullivans and the Jansens.

"I love you." Rafe caught Brooke as she threw herself into his arms. "You promised you would prove to me that you could change, and you couldn't have proved it to me any better than this."

"Actually," he said as he drew back slightly, "there's more."

She had to reach out to caress his jaw with her fingertips. "I don't need anything more than this…than you."

"You deserve more, Brooke. You deserve everything." He picked up the cookbook cover with one hand, and took hers with the other.

Walking through the woods through the fog that was

hovering over the lake felt like being in a dream. One day, she wanted to make love to Rafe right here, in the dark surrounded by the scent of Douglas fir, while the rest of the world slept.

He took her inside her house, and when he closed the front door and deliberately stepped out of the way, she finally saw what she'd missed in her earlier panic at not finding him in the house. The ugly dead bolt was gone. He hadn't put the rusted old lock back on, but while the new lock wasn't tiny, at least it looked like it fit the door.

"I know how difficult it must have been for you to remove the dead bolt." She pressed a soft kiss to his lips. "Thank you."

"Maybe in a few weeks, I'll be able to switch this one out again for an even smaller one."

She laughed out loud at his honesty. It was only natural that the changes he was making would have to come in stages. "I can live with this one."

He put down the recipe book, then pulled the shiny lock pick out of his pocket. "Let's see how long it takes you to pick it."

She couldn't stop smiling as he gestured for her to come back outside with him. She knelt next to him as he showed her the tricks of the P.I. trade. She was amazed he remembered she'd asked to learn how to pick a lock on their first night together.

When he'd said no back then, it was clear that he hadn't wanted to "corrupt" her. So did this mean even more corruption was on the menu?

She really, really hoped it did....

"Your turn now," he said as he handed her the pick.

It was difficult to concentrate with Rafe's thigh pressed against hers and his mouth just inches away, but she forced her brain to focus on the task. Her lower lip between her teeth, she concentrated on each of the steps he'd just run her through.

Less than thirty seconds later, she was amazed when the lock slid open. "Look! I picked the lock on my first try."

Rafe looked between her and the open lock, clearly stunned. "That's the fastest I've ever seen a beginner get a lock open. If I had known how bad my good girl could be…"

She thrilled at the desire beneath his words, but before she could tackle him and show him exactly *how* good being bad with her could be, he was tugging her to her feet and into the kitchen.

"There's more?" It was like following a scavenger hunt where love was the ultimate prize.

He shot her a grin over his shoulder, but she could see that he was a little nervous about whatever he was going to show her next. Rafe brought her to a stop at the edge of the kitchen counter. Two days earlier, they'd made love right in that spot, in the chocolate, and her skin was flushing with remembered heat when she realized there was a blindfold sitting on the counter.

"I'm ready to do that taste test for you now," Rafe told her.

If she didn't already love him, if she hadn't already forgiven him for his mistake, she would have been a goner as he picked up the blindfold and handed it to her. Especially when she could see how hard it was for him to let her take away one of his senses like this.

With trembling hands, she lifted the blindfold up over his head. She kissed him as she slid it in front of his eyes. Fortunately, a batch of her new Summer's

Pleasures recipe was within reach, so she didn't have to move away from him to take one out and put it to his lips. The scrape of his teeth and tongue against her fingertips as he took a bite had her pressing closer to him.

"Delicious."

She couldn't resist licking the chocolate off his lips as she put the rest of the truffle down and took the blindfold off. "So are you."

There was such sweetness to everything he'd done to prove his love to her. Brooke had thought she'd need endless apologies and groveling after the way he'd screwed up. Now she knew that the only thing she needed was Rafe Sullivan exactly as he was—fun and dangerous, light and dark, sweet and sexy, supportive and overprotective, too.

"I never saw my parents argue," she told him. "I never saw them hurt each other in any way. And I never saw passion, either. They always wanted everything to be so perfect, so clean and safe, that I think they were willing to give up true love to make sure they had it. But even if it means I am lacking in common sense, if being without you is what being sensible and making the 'right' decisions means, then I'm happy to keep making the wrong ones. Because I'm not willing to ever give up on true love."

"Do you remember when you asked me what I thought true love was?"

"You looked so shell-shocked, even by the question about *it*," she teased.

"That's because I suddenly realized I was looking right at *it*. Right at you." Now she was the shell-shocked one as he told her, "I thought I had so many smart reasons why we needed to stay away from each other, but all of them boiled down to the same thing—I was afraid to trust anyone. But then there you were on the beach after our first almost-kiss, staring me right in the eye, asking me why I was running. You scared me more than anything ever had in my life. I already knew I wanted to fall asleep with you every night and wake up every morning with you in my arms, but I didn't understand how it could be possible to make a mistake and still find a way to work things out together."

"If you ask me, I think we made it through our tough times even better than we were before."

Bright hope lit his eyes, and how she loved to see it replace the darkness as he made absolutely sure. "Have we?"

"We have." She took his hand and began to draw him back toward the bedroom. "And now I think it's time for us to celebrate."

Being wild, she realized now, wasn't just about sex. It was about wanting Rafe to be her partner in adventures of all kinds—especially the biggest one of all: a love that would last forever.

Of course, she thought with a smile as he scooped her up into his arms and kissed her breathless, she was more than happy to take the wild sex, too.

Rafe could have kissed her all night long, and never wanted to let her go, but there was one more very important thing he needed to give to her, something she had asked for again and again. Relishing the sweet, soft slide of her body against his as he slowly put her down on her feet in the bedroom, he moved his hands to frame her beautiful face.

"What do you say we get a little kinky?"

Her eyes opened wide with surprise, and then such happiness that he knew he'd been a fool to hold out on her for so long.

"You know how badly I want that," she told him, "but only if you want it, too."

Did he ever want it, but first he needed her to understand why he'd held back before. Looking into her eyes gave him the strength to admit, "I was afraid to trust myself with you. I was afraid I wouldn't know when to stop, not just during sex, but after. I was afraid I'd give too much of my heart to you and end up like one of my clients, with it broken in my hands after you were done with me."

Her eyes were soft with emotion, and so much love it floored him. "And now?"

"Now I understand that when passion burns this hot, it's okay to be scared of the power you have over me, the way you turn me inside out with a look, a touch, a kiss." Every word she'd said to him that night at the Italian restaurant when she'd spoken of true love was forever etched on his heart. "Now I know that I can talk to you about absolutely anything, and that you'll still love me. No matter what."

"Always," she promised as she kissed him. "Forever." Her eyes were bright with anticipation when she drew back.

Rafe gave her one last kiss before moving to sit on the soft chair in the corner. "Take your clothes off, sweetheart. Let me see you. All of you."

His breath hitched in his chest as she reached for the belt on her dress. Rafe's heart was beating so hard, his blood roaring so loudly in his ears, that he barely heard the leather falling to the rug. She moved her long hair over one shoulder so that she could pull down the zipper along her spine. The blue fabric slid off her shoulders and hips to puddle on the floor at her feet, and when her bra and panties quickly followed, he thanked God that she wasn't torturing him with a slow striptease tonight.

"How do you want me?"

"Just the way you are." Her answering smile was the brightest he'd seen yet.

Rafe rose up from the chair and took the binding silks out of the dresser without taking his eyes off her incredible beauty. By the time he came to stand in front of her, Brooke's chest was rising and falling rapidly. He lifted one wrist and gently tied one of the silks to it, pressing a kiss to the inside of her palm and then all the way up the inside of her arm. When colorful silk streamed from both wrists, and she was trembling from the path of his kisses across her sensitive skin, he knelt in front of her. Instead of immediately tying the silks to her ankles, he kissed the soft skin across her stomach, her hips, her thighs, moving lower and lower until his mouth was warring with the silks in his hands for the chance to be against her skin.

"Please," she begged. *"More."*

He was going to spend the rest of his life giving her everything she wanted, starting tonight. Lifting her into his arms, he carried her to the bed and laid her down in the center.

"Arms and legs spread, sweetheart."

He'd never dreamed that a woman could be this innocent—and naughty—all at the same time. His hands shook as he tied first her wrists and then her ankles to the bed, and when he was done and she was completely open to him, he knew it was more than her body she was baring, more even than her heart.

Brooke had let him all the way into her soul.

And he was the luckiest man who had ever lived.

Seconds later, he had his clothes off and was kneeling between her thighs as starlight spilled in the bedroom window, illuminating every beautiful curve, every sinful stretch of skin. Her mouth was warm and giving beneath his as he kissed her, and though his lips and hands repeatedly wandered over all of her most sensitive spots, he kept coming back to her lips...and to the kisses that had brought him back to life.

Knowing she trusted him enough to completely let go like this—and that he trusted her enough to completely let go, too—was the most beautiful thing he'd ever experienced.

"I need you, sweetheart."

He quickly untied the silks and as Brooke wrapped her arms and legs around him, with Rafe holding on to her just as tightly, he finally saw that the true love that he'd once thought was as rare as the blue moon had been there all along.

Though Rafe wasn't even close to having his fill of Brooke, for a few precious moments it was enough to hold her in his arms and know that he'd made her happy tonight. Truly happy.

He gazed down in wonder at the beautiful woman beneath him on the bed. "Once upon a time you said I could ask you anything."

"Anything," she confirmed as she wrapped herself tighter around him, her cheek pressed against his.

He'd planned everything else that night, but pure instinct—and love—was what drove him to ask, "Will you marry me, Brooke?"

"Now, that," she said as she lifted her big green eyes to meet his, "sounds truly wild." And then she pressed her lips to his and whispered, *"Yes."*

Epilogue

Later that summer...

"Mom, Dad," Rafe said with Brooke beside him holding his hand, "there's something I want you to have."

Mia made sure to take a picture of the surprise—and utter joy—on her parents' faces at the exact moment they realized Rafe had deeded them the lake house. It was theirs again, only this time no bank could ever take it away from them.

"Rafe? You're giving us the deed for the lake house?" Her mother, Claudia, had tears of joy in her eyes as she pulled her son into a warm hug. "Oh, honey, you're simply amazing."

Her father, Max, wrapped his arms around his wife and his son. "Thank you," he said, his low voice thick with emotion.

Mia sniffled a little, but she refused to cry during the best day she could remember having in years. Along with her parents, all of her brothers except Ian were back at the lake for the weekend. So far they'd been swimming and waterskiing and hiking, and she'd laughed more with her family and her new sister-to-be than she had in a very long time. The sun had set, the bonfire was roaring and they were about to bust out the s'mores when Rafe decided it was finally time to give his parents their anniversary gift.

She'd thought he would do it earlier, but Rafe had seemed a little distracted ever since Brooke had tied her hair back with some really pretty silk scarves after their swim. Lord knew the heat from the way they looked at each other would have been enough to roast the marshmallows even before they'd lit the bonfire. They'd disappeared into the house with some lame excuse that no one bought for a second and hadn't returned to the group on the beach for quite a while.

First her eight cousins had all found love, and now her brother. She had no doubt whatsoever that Rafe and Brooke had what it took to make love last, just like her parents.

Who, she wondered, was going to be next? Adam? Dylan? Ian? Or maybe one of her many cousins on the East Coast?

Just then, Dylan picked up the guitar he'd brought with him and started playing one of her parents' favorite songs, "The Way You Look Tonight." Just as they had when she was a kid, her parents started slow dancing in the sand, the water from the shore lapping over their bare feet. Soon, Rafe and Brooke joined them, so much in love that it was almost hard for Mia to watch them without longing for something that beautiful for herself.

When the song ended, Dylan quickly switched gears from the old standard to a new rock song. Damn it, she thought as the s'more she was eating turned to cement in her stomach, did he have to play *that* song? Even all these years later, Mia couldn't believe she'd been stupid enough to fall for a rock star whom her family and friends never even knew she'd been with....

Her father sat beside her on the log and put his arm around her. "Penny for your thoughts, pumpkin."

Mia knew she should tell her father she was too old for the nickname he'd given her as a little girl. Maybe next year.

"I'm just so happy for Rafe and Brooke, and that her relationship with her parents seems to be a little bit better now, too." The Jansens had spent part of the day at the lake with everyone before heading into Seattle to meet some colleagues for dinner. Things weren't perfect between Brooke and her parents, but Mia could see how much it meant to her friend that they were trying. Just as much as it clearly meant to them that Rafe would obviously give his life for the daughter they'd always protected so carefully.

"Your mother and I are happy for them, too." She could feel her father's warm brown eyes on her. "I've got another penny on me if there's something *you* need to talk to me about."

Mia forced herself to take another bite of her dessert. "Everything's great," she said a little too brightly. "My business has never been better, I'm with my favorite people in the world tonight and I've got a date tomorrow with a hot firefighter I met in town. What more could I want, apart from another s'more?"

But before she could reach for the bag of marshmallows, her father kissed her on the forehead. "I love you, Mia."

The only way to keep from crying on his shoulder was to laugh, which was why instead of roasting her next marshmallow, she tossed it at Adam's head. Seconds later, the campfire erupted into a full-on food fight where no one was safe from flying chocolate or puffed sugar.

Mia had her family, her friends, her career. One day soon, she was going to finally meet a guy who would make her forget all about *him*…and then she'd have everything.

* * * * *

REQUEST YOUR FREE BOOKS!

2 FREE NOVELS
FROM THE ROMANCE COLLECTION
PLUS 2 FREE GIFTS!

YES! Please send me 2 FREE novels from the Romance Collection and my 2 FREE gifts (gifts are worth about $10). After receiving them, if I don't wish to receive any more books, I can return the shipping statement marked "cancel." If I don't cancel, I will receive 4 brand-new novels every month and be billed just $6.24 per book in the U.S. or $6.74 per book in Canada. That's a savings of at least 22% off the cover price. It's quite a bargain! Shipping and handling is just 50¢ per book in the U.S. and 75¢ per book in Canada.* I understand that accepting the 2 free books and gifts places me under no obligation to buy anything. I can always return a shipment and cancel at any time. Even if I never buy another book, the two free books and gifts are mine to keep forever.

194/394 MDN F4XY

Name	(PLEASE PRINT)	
Address		Apt. #
City	State/Prov.	Zip/Postal Code

Signature (if under 18, a parent or guardian must sign)

Mail to the **Harlequin® Reader Service:**
IN U.S.A.: P.O. Box 1867, Buffalo, NY 14240-1867
IN CANADA: P.O. Box 609, Fort Erie, Ontario L2A 5X3

Want to try two free books from another line?
Call 1-800-873-8635 or visit www.ReaderService.com.

* Terms and prices subject to change without notice. Prices do not include applicable taxes. Sales tax applicable in N.Y. Canadian residents will be charged applicable taxes. Offer not valid in Quebec. This offer is limited to one order per household. Not valid for current subscribers to the Romance Collection or the Romance/Suspense Collection. All orders subject to credit approval. Credit or debit balances in a customer's account(s) may be offset by any other outstanding balance owed by or to the customer. Please allow 4 to 6 weeks for delivery. Offer available while quantities last.

Your Privacy—The Harlequin® Reader Service is committed to protecting your privacy. Our Privacy Policy is available online at www.ReaderService.com or upon request from the Harlequin Reader Service.

We make a portion of our mailing list available to reputable third parties that offer products we believe may interest you. If you prefer that we not exchange your name with third parties, or if you wish to clarify or modify your communication preferences, please visit us at www.ReaderService.com/consumerschoice or write to us at Harlequin Reader Service Preference Service, P.O. Box 9062, Buffalo, NY 14269. Include your complete name and address.

BELLA ANDRE

31617	ALWAYS ON MY MIND	___ $7.99 U.S.	___ $8.99 CAN.
31608	COME A LITTLE BIT CLOSER	___ $7.99 U.S.	___ $8.99 CAN.
31600	LET ME BE THE ONE	___ $7.99 U.S.	___ $8.99 CAN.
31560	IF YOU WERE MINE	___ $7.99 U.S.	___ $8.99 CAN.
31559	I ONLY HAVE EYES FOR YOU	___ $7.99 U.S.	___ $8.99 CAN.
31558	CAN'T HELP FALLING IN LOVE	___ $7.99 U.S.	___ $8.99 CAN.
31557	FROM THIS MOMENT ON	___ $7.99 U.S.	___ $9.99 CAN.
31556	THE LOOK OF LOVE	___ $5.99 U.S.	___ $5.99 CAN.

(limited quantities available)

TOTAL AMOUNT	$ _____
POSTAGE & HANDLING	$ _____
($1.00 for 1 book, 50¢ for each additional)	
APPLICABLE TAXES*	$ _____
TOTAL PAYABLE	$ _____

(check or money order—please do not send cash)

To order, complete this form and send it, along with a check or money order for the total amount, payable to Harlequin MIRA, to: **In the U.S.:** 3010 Walden Avenue, P.O. Box 9077, Buffalo, NY 1426-9077; **In Canada:** P.O. Box 636, Fort Erie, Ontario, L2A 5X3.

Name: _____

Address: _____ City: _____

State/Prov.: _____ Zip/Postal Code: _____

Account Number (if applicable): _____

075 CSAS

*New York residents remit applicable sales taxes.
*Canadian residents remit applicable GST and provincial taxes.

HARLEQUIN® MIRA®
www.Harlequin.com

MBA0914BL